Elektrik

Elektrik

Caribbean Writing

CALICO

Elektrik is eighth in the Calico Series.

Two Lines Press
582 Market Street, Suite 700, San Francisco, CA 94104
www.twolinespress.com

ISBN: 978-1-949641-50-9

Library of Congress Cataloging-in-Publication Data available upon request.

Cover design by Crisis
Typesetting and interior design by LOKI
Printed in the United States of America

THIS BOOK WAS PUBLISHED WITH SUPPORT
FROM THE NATIONAL ENDOWMENT FOR THE ARTS.

MIREILLE JEAN-GILLES

Voracious street

*

The missing

*

In the unwearied
heart of the sea

TRANSLATED BY ERIC FISHMAN

Où commence la Caraïbe?
Où finit-elle?

Voracious street

Woman with large hoops

I always see her on the same street, climbing-descending, sitting in a chair or on the grass (the *turf* as we used to say), standing up, walking, she's large, beautiful, a stately bearing, walks through the streets in large midi dresses that she lightly lifts to ease her stride, I never see her without her rings, I often watch her, stare at her, does she know why, does she know she's beautiful, so naturally beautiful that I don't know if she knows she's beautiful, besides her ease, her assurance, nothing lets on (her hoops) nothing lets on that she knows she's beautiful, she walks, stands out against the scenery, the sky her parasol, her rings glitter in the sun, nothing suggests she knows she's beautiful, since she's always natural with her stay-at-home dresses and her hair up in two puffs: how Black women do their hair when they stay home (truth be told the town was her home), a woman who knows she's beautiful is always tempted to force her beauty with some artifice, as for her, she doesn't need anything to be beautiful, as she perhaps knows, she always walks through town in the same style, no need to hang around those places you go to show off your beauty, for being beautiful to have meaning, not her, she needs nothing, so she stays in the street, takes a seat from time to time, facing the Sky, immensity...

Fishermen's ball

The difference between a *bourgeoise*, a well-born woman from town, and a woman from the countryside? Well, when the woman from the countryside dances, well, the more she ages the more she dances (unchains herself), the more she moves about, the more you sense that she has gathered experience each day, (each night), each year.

The *bourgeoise*, the more she ages, the less she dances, the less she grooves, it would seem she no longer has any feeling in her body, that she will have spent her life mastering it, and in the end (at least in appearance, since she will have learned above all to *appear*), it will become nothing more than a bit of dead wood.

Group of women by the sea

They seem to wander,
    walking slowly
      resigned
    as if Time had passed by
  forgetting them along the edge of the path
They go out in a group,
  go on cruises,
    go to mass,
      go to the sea
        where they pass by like shadows...

Still, what marvels
  do these bodies hide
      weighed down with an entire life,
     what fiery loves
      have they sheltered?

  But their bodies are weary
    weary of being here still
    of soon being here no more...

  But...among all these women coming out of the water,

which was beautiful
(cruel)
and deadly?

One, yes, surely...

In Fort-de-France

In Fort-de-France, the women aren't more beautiful than elsewhere in Martinique, but since they're in town, they walk, and so they fully express their beauty.

*

She walks in such a haughty manner, such a proud manner, such a superior manner, down a Fort-de-France street, that I ask myself *Who* is she meeting in Fort-de-France? *Who*, in Fort-de-France, could possibly have the honor and privilege of meeting *Her*?

Someone should come up with a contest for the day's most beautiful woman in Fort-de-France and give her an award (to reimburse her for the ruinous energy it takes to be beautiful). This morning, the most beautiful was a kind of matador: a long, flared denim skirt, denim top too, leaving bare (as required) one to two centimeters of midriff. She was walking, flying, everyone was looking at her, she had a phone in her hand and was speaking with a firm, assured voice, giving the impression that you could refuse her nothing, that nature—and men—had given her everything...

*

She was pink from head to toe, bag, dress, everything was pink, nail polish, eye shadow, lipstick, blush, everything was pink from head to toe, this elegant woman in a thousand shades of pink could only be Martinican...

*

All these women have a mystery, a depth: Beauty's secret.

*

She was walking in a street without a sidewalk as if she were strolling on a stage. Alone, she was walking along that street under the midday sun, with all the drivers as her audience.

*

She was walking slowly, full of determination. She seemed to possess the power and cold calm of felines: no woman could have competed with her...

*

A shapely woman, same shapes, same width, yellow pants, which made her even wider, gold hoops, and then it was her, it was really her, the one who drew attention all the way to Fort-de-France, where women are beautiful, she walked, attracted gazes, lived off these gazes, and then, satiated, turned back home, toward the Mountain...

The missing

I don't know whether to speak of her in the present or the past, since I don't know if she's still alive. She no longer responds to my letters, and I don't dare to call her, afraid she'll have died in the meantime and I'll end up dialing the beyond. I like relationships with *crazy* women but not with *dead* ones. So I remain in this uncertainty, one way to make her immortal.

I haven't seen her since I left Guiana. Later she left "for France," as she put it. She seemed tired of life. Leaving Guiana was like sitting down in the antechamber of death. She was done making relationships with the living; any future on Earth was already in her past. And I heard no more from her.

H. was simply a friend, but arriving in Martinique, I understood that the béké was a separate species, these white folks whose shadows projected on the ground reveal the gaping wounds of a history that, it seems, they don't deny. They were only an instrument of History. As for us, we were, and are still, on the wrong side, hence our resentment, which they pretend not to understand.

H. wasn't a representation of history to me. She was an old white woman, playful and lively. I spent entire hours listening to her, and I imagined myself in her stories. Her father, a mining engineer in the age of the gold rush, had been "trapped" in the Guianese forest by a Black servant's "artful skill," and had had two illegitimate sons from her that he had nonetheless recognized, who then went off to live as mulâtres in Martinique.

H. often talked about her husband, from the American South, proud of being a WASP, in other words proud of not having a single drop of Black blood in his veins. She told me that at the age of forty, in order to measure up to the ideal of the American woman, she'd had to dye her hair blonde and even... wear miniskirts.

H. talked about her ancestors, among the first colonizers to arrive in Guiana in the seventeenth century. They transformed the swampy lands into polders. There's nothing like slavery to achieve such feats, at a time when religion and humanism denied us man's fate, before returning us, in a forced march, into the ranks of Humanity.

H. told me about her ancestors' lives in a completely innocent and bucolic way, people who concerned themselves with the health of their slaves, who kept entire notebooks, which she still had, on various methods for healing them, like a farmer would have done for his livestock. All this wasn't shocking: it was so far away, and H. so charming.

In Martinique, on the other hand, past and present ceaselessly collide, the colonizers haven't changed inside or out, so how could we not think they regard us as they did three centuries ago, as slaves who deserve irons.

H. spoke to me frequently of the béké women that she met when she went to visit her brothers in Fort-de-France, women she found particularly disagreeable. I didn't know what to say personally on this topic, as I'd never had the chance to rub shoulders with them, except in line, at the François supermarket where they came to do their shopping. And everything I knew about them I had read in a book of (hi)stories, including that for centuries they've lived in a "fortress under siege" by mulâtresses, capresses, and other Black women who've driven their husbands wild, which over the course of this history must have made them absolutely *crazy*, hysterical, permanently on the verge of nervous breakdowns.

H. never spoke Creole. Only a French from *France* té ka soti di so bouch'. I cannot recall a single moment when Guianese Creole deformed her mouth.

In Martinique, on the other hand, the colonizer distills Creole, he revels in Creole. It's so beautiful when a béké speaks Creole, in crowds in the shallows. The fascination for the executioner is at its peak.

In the unwearied heart of the sea

Where does the Caribbean begin? Where does it end?

Was it born in the imagination of fifteenth-century explorers? Did it exist before? Does it exist now?

The Caribbean is an "atopia," you say. Now you want it to be a "utopia," a poetic construction to escape the cliché of human destruction.

Does the Caribbean exist?

My consciousness of being Caribbean is limited to the simplest expression: a place that lives in me, and that I unfurl, like a nomad his tent, in each place where I live.

But then there's "the other place." Now that schools have introduced several infamous doses of the founding crimes of their Caribbean, to compensate for this disaster, "the other place" strives every day to remind us "what we are" and "what we are not."

So, as for "the other place," the other day I was saying: "My God, what a disaster, the arrival of television on the Maroni River, where all these Indians and Africans live whom they've struggled to assimilate, to strip of all notion of themselves." So, I was saying, "My God (surely theirs), what a disaster, this appearance of the screen in this world, another world." Since the very thing they had such difficulty doing, despite their police, their churches, their schools, their languages, their social security payments, well, with "the other place," they will finally be able to do it: reduce the Caribbean to a place without memory, and make each of us carry the heavy burden of a lost world.

So, has the Caribbean existed? Does it exist? Could it exist?

Can poetry, in an increasingly virtual world, shore up the borders of our Caribbean?

*

I've seen a gathering of white birds flying over endless lines of cars, cars that couldn't go anywhere and yet make men proud—faster than birds—soaring.

Always this airport runway, the birds always there to rival the planes.

The dancer is beautiful, and poignant, like all beauty. She can neither fly nor fly away.

The summits swoon in and out of the clouds.

To work in this place is a monastic practice, in other words you must work alone, for a long time, in darkness, see a light, share it with no one, be in shadow, stained by darkness, go to the depths of yourself, and go forward always with this flame, this hope that drives me toward an unknown destination, but one where I will assuredly, certainly arrive.

They will never abolish daybreak, this morning of mornings, such a morning daybreak, they can never make the sun rise at noon, and this is reassuring.

I would like to abolish the "I," but I can't manage it.

What are clouds under the Caribbean sky?

What do they bring?
What do they carry away?

Are they going far from here, far over there, far off, those who are making it so that, beneath the Caribbean sky, the only thing left of the Caribbean is the sea—and for how much longer?

Sulimé-Anacaona despairs in front of her mirror.

Sulimé-Anacaona plunges, hangs onto several given dreams.
Sulimé-Anacaona surges to the surface, plunges, and weeps.
Sulimé-Anacaona despairs of her mirror.

The little girls on the sides of roads, students with their backpacks, are, along roads, paths, and highways, like wildflowers blooming from the earth, for better or worse, from the sugar cane fields.

In the morning, at daybreak, they went looking for water, they went along the paths, legs firm, heads high, they went each morning, before sunrise, to look for water, far, quite far from their homes. It was said they had beautiful legs because of the hills.

In the morning, I see them along the roads, going where, nowhere. You have to get up early, very early, before daybreak, in order to run. Frantic race toward beauty, since today being beautiful is more essential than water, so, to get up at daybreak, this unwearied dream of being beautiful, very beautiful, remains.

Let the image of these women with their children ripen, intertwined at the edge of the road. In the Caribbean, these bodies of mothers, attached to their children, always retain the tired signs of past embraces.

Let me dance,
Let me therefore dance like Sulimé-Anacaona.
Between sun and sea, rhyme, swim, seize words, join the parts one by one, and go out dancing...

I would like to be beautiful for my Husband, like Sulimé-Anacaona, to be always wondrous and wondering, to be there and take over the space, with each breath call attention, with each movement provoke emotion, with each smile make the world collapse...

The Caribbean is a God, her head in the sky, crowned in stars, and in men desperately searching for their gods who have been hunted from the earth, and are perhaps hidden somewhere in the Caribbean Sea.

I remember, the other day, these young girls chirping and babbling with their only concern: to iridate the world with their beauty.

I had left the road to sit by a marina, a forgotten place and perhaps the prefiguration of what our Caribbean will be tomorrow, when we'll be, here in our Caribbean, relegated to the status of decor for travelers come from the sea.

So, here in this forgotten place, I was in the middle of despairing for our lost Caribbean, when, suddenly, a thunderous music took over the space. I was instantly pulled from disabused daydreams. But it was already too late, the car was gone as quickly as it had arrived: a lightning vision.

The Caribbean, unable to fully exist, is frequently reduced to a state of lightning visions, as when, for example, Sulimé-Anacaona's nanny told me unbelievable stories. Despite having been relinquished to "the other place," I was impressed by her abilities of imagination (or resistance) when she assured me that so-and-so is a "Dorlys" and that, as proof, he had come to visit her the other evening, and from then on, to protect herself, she slept with her underwear inside out, or again that such-and-such person in the highlands of the hills holds "séances," and that another had stepped over a snake without touching it, but that had been enough to paralyze him anyways...

And I could write entire pages on what they call "our good old beliefs," which, regardless of their own existence, make us exist, uncover for us a face of our Caribbean soul.

And then, there's this other lightning vision, but you can live this one as often as you want, since you have to pass the same place again and again in your car to welcome it deeply and powerfully, like any lightning vision. This seller of Haitian fruits who, in a spot in Fort-de-France, almost a crossroads, sells her fruits, but it's her entire being that's offered, and her island as well, she is so beautiful, ceaselessly descending and climbing the path, her buttocks moving with assurance and firmness, lighting vision of our water carriers from long ago, the fruit seller endlessly reminds us that stripping someone down doesn't only lead to beauty of the soul.

Public beautification projects aren't eligible for European loans, unless they're going to restore the facades of houses to make them more agreeable to the eyes of tourists.

I give in, the ground sinks, I lose myself, search for myself, and drown in myself, I swim, float, the ground becomes unstable, ready to engulf me, my girls exhaust me, and I sink into myself, and slide, and fall, and pick myself up, stand up, and bedrock, jolt, I fall asleep, exhaust myself, I lie down, and I cannot get up, wash myself, perfume myself, cannot be beautiful like my girls who fill me, fill the void they've created around me...

Punctuated void...because "Love me," you said, "and nothing but me," you said...

The Caribbean, this "punctuated void," you said, reminds me of that town that I looked for in vain the other day and that exists only in its past, its failed rendezvous with history, its broken dreams of splendor, its future irremediably turned toward an absence, toward a lack, toward an end that could only have been reached in a past era.

The Caribbean echoes like a lost world, a stolen world, a world that exists only in this intense feeling of disappearance, of destruction, of a perfect crime with its victims as its ultimate creation! Don't depend on me to praise the Caribbean, the apology for the crime, when, to my Sulimé-Anacaona, I have no other god to offer but Theirs, with thorns on his head, and on his hands the blood of Anacaona and all the gods he buried within me...

Wander in the Caribbean Sea, struggle rather than fight, since the other has found refuge in me, put him beyond the walls, swim, search for a rock where you can breathe and return the beauty buried in the sea of blood...

Struggle rather than fight, since the other has found refuge in me, his language is in my mouth, an impure blood flows in my veins, baroque tales live in my head, and only my heart fights, more than struggles, to keep my Caribbean Guiana in this body that brought Sulimé-Anacaona into the world.

Up there, you definitively put away all these books that had so nourished us when it was still a dream, an attainable dream, to chase them away, far from here.

Poetry was confiscated by the word mumblers.
May she be given back to the world!

May the Caribbean Sea carry all these verses, which carry them,
transport them, bring them elsewhere, far from here...

May the Caribbean Sea welcome the poem as ultimate and
sublime utopia...

I want to be a green leaf,
to drink water and the salts of life,
without the pretention of any flower,
not even that of she who,
like the town where I was born,
is called Cayenne...

The dancer desperately wants to embrace beauty... The closer
she gets, the more it pulls away...

GAËL OCTAVIA

African Mask

TRANSLATED BY KAIAMA L. GLOVER

Elle avance maintenant avec l'impression d'être une elfe, enfin gracieuse, affranchie de la pesanteur.

THE PLANE WAS LATE. AND THEN THERE WERE THE TRAFFIC jams, perfectly normal for a Saturday at that time, heading out to the beaches. Though immobilized for far too long in Cousin Raoul's convertible (Raoul was the one who'd done well for himself in life), on that stretch of the state highway they call the "freeway" around here, the guests had no problem with the sun. They'd be showing up for lunch, faces flushed, with a touch of sunstroke.

Frédérique hadn't been waiting for them. She was busy getting beaten at ping pong by her little eleven-year-old cousin. No one was waiting for them, really. They'd all been gorging themselves on spicy blood sausage, savory patties, ham and pineapple, and whatever else gets served with pre-lunch drinks in December. The kids had gone back to roughhousing in the pool, except for Sarah, who was caught up in a never-ending phone conversation about the boys she liked, about the boys she might like, about the boys she didn't like. Aunts and uncles busied themselves with various activities. Only Aunt

Gilda had been pacing back and forth watching the red gate, because she'd spent the entire morning cooking and liked each dish to be eaten at the optimal temperature.

There were enough little cousins around that day for Frédérique and Sarah—fifteen-year-old twins as different from one another as two sisters can possibly be—not to end up relegated to the kids' table. Instead, they found themselves seated facing the main attraction: the actor freshly arrived from Paris, accompanied by his very beautiful wife.

Cousin Raoul (the one who'd done well for himself in life) was an elegant, smooth-talking thirty-year-old who had made friends with an incredible assortment of people. A family defect, Frédérique sometimes said to herself, thinking of her mother, who'd go up to just about anyone in line at the supermarket—except that Raoul, an extensive traveler, had the gift of stumbling upon exiled writers, avant-garde artists, ill-fated filmmakers, legendary jazz musicians, and other fascinating characters. And whenever they traveled to Martinique, they always took him up on his invitation to join one of his gargantuan family meals.

The actor played the role of distinguished guest to perfection. He spoke modestly of his profession, affirming—while knowing full well that no one believed him—that it was just like any other job. His wife interrupted him every once in a while to share some funny story or another. He was Nigerian. The wife, German. They each spoke French with a different accent. The aunts and uncles let out little gasps of appreciation, laughed too loudly. They asked a hundred questions, all of which an embarrassed Frédérique found idiotic.

She stayed quiet throughout lunch, discreetly observing the couple, while Sarah squirmed in her seat and shot the actor sly looks, full of longing. Frédérique examined every aspect of the man's face, that African face that was nothing like other Black faces you'd see around there. She inspected his wide forehead, crowned with a robust Afro that stood straight up like a field of cane and glistened like onyx. She noted the imperfect skin on his chin and cheeks, a razor-burned contrast to the smoothness of his forehead. She followed the curve of his majestic aquiline nose and stopped at the full lips that barely revealed his impeccable ivory teeth.

After the meal, instead of lying around the pool as had been proposed, the guests wanted to go "for a walk in the forest." The two teenagers and the string of little cousins joined the expedition. Raoul led the herd. Aunts and uncles stayed behind to nap. The lovely German threw on a pair of khaki shorts and a safari jacket. Frédérique suddenly recalled that forgotten old portrait of her great-grandfather in his white helmet, now gathering dust in some storage room full of colonial treasures, among statuettes made of precious materials. They headed off merrily, shaking off the midday drowsiness with the help of raucous children's walking tunes like "one mile more, it wears 'em down, it wears 'em down"— military tunes sung at the top of their lungs.

The "forest" consisted of swampy woodlands that made the German woman regret her khaki shorts, since she lacked the one weapon that would have been useful in that context: mosquito repellent. The smile she'd been wearing since their arrival had faded slightly. Between her white tennis shoes sinking into the mud and the loud slaps she was giving her thighs, she looked less like a sophisticated beauty than like a clown in the middle of an act.

Frédérique let out a cruel little laugh. The mangrove was her element. She moved with the agility of a monkey across the slippery ground and through the brambles that scratched at her skin. The actor held his own, fully adapting to the heat and mosquitos. He seemed delighted by the unusual vegetation. Frédérique reminded herself that he'd only known Lagos, New York, London, Tokyo, Berlin, Paris. He was probably one of those city folk, full of nostalgia for unspoiled nature and fantasies of a return to life in the wild. He didn't seem at all worried about his wife, all the way at the rear of the pack, behind the cousins. He walked quickly, stopping only to contemplate the flora and fauna, occasionally asking Raoul for botanical information. Frédérique burned with a desire to answer him herself—she knew every tree, every liana, every rhizome—but her shyness walled her up in silence, like some kind of wildling. Having stolen a glance at the wife, whom Sarah had taken by the arm to help her along the increasingly wet path, she tried to pick up the pace, passing ahead of Raoul.

The acceleration was intoxicating. A strange shiver ran through her from head to toe. She had to stop. Running her hand over her torso, she realized she was bathed in sweat. The voices of the others were getting closer. Without turning around, Frédérique focused on the melodic sound of the actor's Nigerian accent. She began walking again. She felt like a sprite as she moved forward, graceful at last, weightless. She imagined the actor behind her, noticing her for the first time that day, admiring her light step, her fluid movements, her perfect harmony with the enchanted surroundings. With the pressure of each footstep on the soft earth, she felt a peculiar energy spreading up through her calves and thighs, and then exploding, radiating throughout her entire body.

She was still heady with the promenade when they got back. She went to shut herself up in the bathroom adjoining the vast space they called the "kids' room"—a sort of dormitory, with mattresses strewn about, that took up the entire third floor of the immense family home. There, the intoxication suddenly vanished.

Her own fifteen years looked nothing like Sarah's. Her twin, who had entered puberty early, flaunted a set of breasts like two juicy pears, a wasp's waist of a silhouette, a derrière that turned the heads of grown men as often as those of boys their age. Frédérique passed her hand lightly over the two buds of her own chest, darker than the rest of her skin but hardly sticking out at all. She pinched her barely noticeable waist, her skinny thighs. Her thick eyebrows were bushy. Her kinky, tangled hair fell to her shoulders in uneven locks. She could just as easily have been a fine-featured young Bob Marley fanboy. It was the mangrove that had dazed her earlier, all the better to fool her. That gaze she'd felt at her back, so ardent, so palpable—that gaze had been an illusion. The actor probably hadn't even been aware of her existence.

Hit with the burning stream of water from the shower, she nonetheless felt a return of the current that had passed through her in the mangrove. She redirected the showerhead —made the feeling last by mentally sketching the irregular surface of those cheeks, the aquiline nose, the ivory teeth.

She couldn't help comparing that feeling to the sad memory of an afternoon three months earlier. A bed with creaky springs. Science fiction film posters on the walls.

Jeremy. His breath, his smell, his teenage awkwardness. She quickly chased all of that from her thoughts.

Back to the mangrove, the trees, the actor so nearby. Eyes closed, Frédérique prolonged the dance of the showerhead, its wet, hot caress—until Sarah started banging on the door. *What was she doing in there? Since when do people lock doors in this immodest family where everyone has seen everyone else naked, at least once if not twice?* Frédérique jumped, turned off the water, quickly dried herself. Sarah was still grumbling when she opened the door. *Showering for all that time? Did she think the hot water never ran out?*

Then it was time to go down to the table. Frédérique had been seated far away from the actor, on Aunt Gilda's authority, whereas Sarah had the honor of sitting just to his right—the lovely German had gone to lie down after the walk and would miss dinner. Once again, the man overflowed with charm. He treated Sarah like a proper lady, served her wine despite the protestations of her aunts. Frédérique felt cursed. Sarah doubled down on the sly looks, rested her pretty chin on her closed fist. The Nigerian didn't seem bothered by her ridiculous simpering. Frédérique raged inside. She wanted to get as far away as possible from the table full of people talking too much, laughing too much, standing between her and the man— between her and the feeling of the mangrove—like a sonic and visual wall, a field of static interference. She tried to focus on the man's voice, like during the walk. She conjured up the wet earth of the path, the wide leaves, the branches crisscrossing the narrow passages, but in vain. The feeling was gone.

Later that night, Frédérique rushed to claim the mattress situated alongside the back wall of the kids' room, right beneath the window. That way she would be sleeping just above the bed in the guest bedroom on the second floor. Sarah chose the mattress next to hers and tried to tell her about her dinner, recounting every word the Nigerian man had spoken, clucking on without realizing that, this time, there could be no complicity between them. Frédérique pretended to snore so that her sister would be quiet.

She remained awake, though, alert to the noises of the house. She didn't want to miss the moment when the actor, who was sipping a last glass of aged rum with Raoul, went to bed. At last, there was silence. The adults gave in to their fatigue. Frédérique started off by rubbing her body with her index finger while imagining the man just below her, separated from her by a bit of empty space and concrete. Little by little, she dared to knead her own flesh, mentally removing the space between her and him. Flush with the blood boiling within her, her chest inflated. Her hands retraced the paths of her curves. The illusion of feeling her own body that way, sculpted, feminine, sensual, heightened the audacity—the voluptuousness—of her movements. She didn't ever want to stop, fought against her sleepiness, kept it all from dissipating. She didn't even stop herself when she suddenly heard Sarah's voice, whispering a few cryptic words in her dreams. The window was open. Frédérique breathed in the air with delight, imagining that it came from the Nigerian man's mouth. When she finally fell asleep, it was with the man's breath on her tongue.

The sky was still radiant on Sunday. Raoul announced that they'd all be heading to the beach. He chose one that was known for its rough waves. Frédérique knew she'd be as clumsy in the water as she'd been at ease in the thick greenery. And first thing that morning, while the bathroom mirror had restored her androgynous physique, she'd watched Sarah slip on a red bikini that emphasized the fullness of her breasts and the roundness of her bottom. Frédérique decided not to go, to stay behind on her own, to think about the mangrove, to take advantage of the silence to bring back the strange feeling—with the help of a few caresses and the memory of the walk through the wet earth.

As she waited for everyone to leave, she took a seat at the old, out-of-tune piano in the second-floor living room. She was the only one who used it every now and again. She'd be forgiven for missing the beach if it was to stay home and practice piano. The family was proud of her musical talents.

Impatient, she massacred Chopin. After five minutes, some-one entered the room.

"Are you the one playing so beautifully, young lady?" asked the actor, a decidedly perfect specimen, adding that she'd been playing his favorite waltz.

He had come up to look for a mask, fins, and snorkel. She told him he wouldn't be able to see anything in the swirling waves.

"You're not coming with us, young lady?" he lamented, without giving up on the equipment.

She hesitated, closed the piano, and answered that yes, of course she was coming.

At the beach, the aunts and uncles remained prudently on the sand, underneath their umbrellas, while the cousins braved the waves. The Nigerian and his wife—who was back to her smiling, beautiful self—disappeared beneath the walls of water only to reappear, screaming like little children. Sarah paraded about in her bikini for a few minutes before throwing herself into the water, too.

Frédérique hadn't even deigned to undress. She grabbed the voluminous novel she'd hurriedly stashed in her beach bag and stretched out on a towel at some distance from the adults. A second folded towel served as a pillow, so she was able to observe the actor while hiding behind her book. They were playing a game now. A wrestling game that consisted of catching one another, pushing each other over, throwing each other into the waves. All of a sudden, the man, his wife, Sarah, and one of the cousins came out of the water. They rushed toward her. By the time Frédérique caught on, it was too late; she was being lifted up, carried by each of her four limbs. The actor was holding fast to one of her thighs. The searing intensity of the contact was paralyzing. An even more powerful current than the one she'd felt at the mangrove traveled up to her belly.

The game continued in the water. The actor kept pressing her against him to better launch her into the trough of a wave. Once. Twice. They were only furtive embraces, but each one of them would stay burned into her forever. The feeling of the man's torso, as it caressed her budding breasts through her soaking-wet polo shirt, was exquisitely violent. Everything inside her contracted, quivered, then released in a sigh. The third time, she was sucked into a rolling swell. She let herself be tossed about, offering herself up completely to the force of the wave. It felt like a continuation of his embrace, the force of the water mixed up with that of the man. She swallowed a glassful, savoring it like a kiss. When she finally emerged, it was to let herself drift, sated and yet completely empty.

They finally headed back. No songs or chitchat in Raoul's car. The sea had tired everyone out. Frédérique stared at the nape of the Nigerian's neck. He was seated just in front of her. Could he feel her gaze?

One of her little cousins had rested his head on her lap. He was the youngest of the bunch, the most adorable one. She smiled at him tenderly. It was then that she realized that, as far as the actor was concerned, she was only a child. Even Sarah in her red bikini was only a child to him. At most, he might have felt some slight affection for them—nothing for his wife to worry about. They were little girls he could roughhouse with in perfect innocence.

Arriving at the house, they sat down at the table to enjoy Aunt Gilda's marvels one last time. Frédérique knew that the family would head back to Fort-de-France by nightfall. The guests would stay on for a few extra days of vacation, but she'd never see them again.

The following Monday, Frédérique met up with Jeremy at the schoolyard gates when classes got out. She asked if he wanted to walk home together. Jeremy nodded his head, incredulous. She hadn't spoken a word to him in three months.

They'd known one another since kindergarten. Jeremy was the only boy in the neighborhood to have set his sights on her, whereas all the others were lovesick over her sister— her bewitching face, her hair cascading down the middle of her back, and of course, her insolent curves. Frédérique felt a mixture of sisterly affection and light disdain for Jeremy. Nonetheless, at the beginning of the previous school year they'd decided to settle the tedious matter of their virginity together.

Sarah had lost hers already during that summer break with a pretty boy who was just about legal age. She'd been dreaming about it for more than two years and told her twin sister that it had all gone exactly as she'd hoped. She'd spared her none of the details: the young man's impressive morphology, the pain—the worst she'd ever felt—that had ended just as it began, the pleasure that had suffused her and left her half dead. Embellished by flourishes and metaphors likely borrowed from romance novels, her sister's story left Frédérique feeling skeptical—but she'd gone along with it nonetheless, so as not to contradict her. To tell the truth, matters of the heart hadn't held much interest for her. In the past few years, she'd watched as hormones took over all her friends and turned them into ravenous creatures, in thrall to the opposite sex, waiting around, analyzing the tiniest signs from those everyone agreed were the most handsome or charismatic. She, however, remained indifferent to their powers. She thought of herself as above all that nonsense. Sarah said she was cold, unfeeling—swore she was missing something. But Frédérique had no desire to change. Maybe sometimes she'd envied that state of euphoria her sister and her friends could be plunged into by a kiss, a word, a glance—but she congratulated herself on keeping such alienating, debilitating things at bay. Her joy, her pleasure, didn't depend on anyone else's good will. Especially not those boys who only cared about "that" (yes, that's also what everyone said), trying every form of coercion to make you give in and then leaving you to your sad fate once they'd had their way.

Sarah's experience had nonetheless titillated her curiosity. She'd thought about it for several days, wondering to what extent what her sister had told her was true. What could they possibly have been like, those surges of pleasure that had supposedly shaken her body, that had set every fiber of her being aquiver, from the surface of her skin to her most intimate depths? And how had that pretty boy made all of her senses rejoice, as she'd claimed? Frédérique had repeated Sarah's words to herself. How she'd described the contact of her skin with his, and all the ways they'd caressed one another, rubbed one another, pinched, licked, bitten one another, the words they'd murmured to each other, their breathing, their sighs. Everything was studded with incredible colors, sounds, odors, textures, tastes. Unforgettable, Sarah had assured her. Frédérique had tried to imagine this prodigious thing. In the secrecy of her bedroom, she had groped at her own body, looking for some mysterious region she hadn't been aware of—the entryway to that parallel universe Sarah had explored. She went after it to no avail. Everything remained dreadfully abstract.

The best way to settle the matter would be to try it, she told herself. Once the idea had taken root in her mind, she'd wanted to execute it quickly. She had the good fortune of having Jeremy right there.

So it had been she who called him, she who'd bluntly proposed the idea of "doing it" at his place while his parents were out—right there on the bed where in the past they'd sat in perfect innocence while playing Monopoly or pinochle with their respective sisters, or done whatever, just hanging out together, lazily listening to some Jamaican tune without making the slightest effort to stave off the chronic ennui of adolescence.

"How about Wednesday afternoon at three?" she'd suggested before hanging up without even giving him a chance to respond. She knew that—despite his leading-man looks; despite his height, his swimmer's musculature; and despite, above all, his bronze skin and green eyes, so appreciated at school—the painfully shy Jeremy had never touched a girl. She'd given him no room to waver, showing up at his house at three o'clock sharp. And so, they'd done it. And Frédérique had pretty much felt nothing, not even pain. Only the condom spattered with whitish fluid and tossed next to the bed by an exhausted Jeremy proved to her that anything had happened. But the colors, the textures, the odors, the tastes were even more abstract than before. Disappointed, but unable to share her disappointment with Jeremy, she'd avoided him for three months.

That Monday after meeting the Nigerian, on the road home from school, Frédérique and Jeremy started off walking in silence. Then she struck up a conversation. Jeremy was terse. He was wary, wondering whether to expect some new mood swing, some new about-face. But he was moved, too. Happy she'd reestablished contact. She told him about her weekend, unable to stop herself from mentioning the actor, whose memory still shook her—but without overdoing it, so he wouldn't notice anything. They arrived at his house. The garage was empty. His parents were out. He invited her in for a soda.

In the bedroom, she insisted on covering the closed shutters with opaque fabric. She wanted total darkness. And then they threw themselves at each other. She could keep her eyes open without completely seeing Jeremy's face, with its too-delicate features, or the childish posters on his walls. She avoided caressing his wavy hair, impossible to pass for that of the Nigerian. But Jeremy's body would do the trick this time. Frédérique was electrified by his touch, by the taste of him and his slightly acidic cologne. She was seeing the green and brown of the mangrove, smelling the odor of the earth engorged with water. In their panting breath she could hear the rustling of the branches and leaves. She also heard his Nigerian accent, retraced his aquiline nose, licked his lips, banged her own teeth against his ivory teeth. After a few minutes, the feeling she thought had been lost—the feeling came back to her. She let herself be carried away on its miraculous swell.

They went at it nearly every day, in one of their bedrooms or the other, depending on their parents' comings and goings, and wherever else seemed possible—outdoors or in out-of-the-way places safe from prying eyes. If there was any light, Frédérique would close her eyes. Or else she let the shadows fool her, persuading herself that the body on top of her, underneath her, was the Nigerian's. Jeremy stopped being surprised by her insatiability. Her voraciousness made him proud. His own pleasure was heightened by the idea that, from then on, he'd managed to satisfy her every time.

They kept their secret from everyone, even their sisters. No one suspected anything. Sarah had a new lover. Frédérique listened to her recount their antics using the same phrases she'd used to talk about her pretty boy from summer break. She looked at Sarah condescendingly, convinced that her twin sister knew nothing, and would never know anything, about those waves that turn time upside down for the moment of an embrace and then leave you floating on the surface of the waters. She even ended up convincing herself that she alone truly knew what pleasure was.

They kept it up for a year, then she fell in love, for real, with another boy. With the one she loved, the first time was a disaster. She was so disappointed, she burst into tears. The boy was taken aback. He questioned her. He got angry. She reassured him, swore to him: it was the orgasm, yes, the orgasm that made her cry. But she was worried. She had thought naively that being in love would make things different—that the feeling would arise on its own, that she'd never have to use the trick of the Nigerian actor again.

A few days later, they tried again. She closed her eyes and fantasized. Like with Jeremy, the trick worked. She rediscovered the colors, the odors, the swell, the final release.

When the boy she loved left her, she found another. Then another. With each of them it was the same thing: She needed total darkness and the image of the Nigerian, otherwise nothing happened. So she realized she'd been bewitched.

The image of that afternoon in the mangrove ultimately became blurry, as if buried somewhere deep in her memory. But there were still the trees, the heat, her agility on the muddy path, her thrill at knowing she was being looked at. And then the feeling, that explosion within her, which he'd injected into her without even touching her, with his Yoruba Magi's power, and which now condemned her to forever depend on him.

She decided to fight it. She multiplied her conquests and experiences with boys, with girls, to the point of frightening Sarah, who'd become oddly well behaved—as if the fact of being twins meant they could by no means behave the same way, too. She tried to erase the actor's image and retain only the feeling, to coil up in the trough of a wave, letting herself be tossed about like a disjointed puppet in its swells. But it was as if the wave never really wanted her, always leaving her standing up, feet planted in the sand. In the end, she gave up. She gave into him, into his power.

Years went by. Boys, and then men, followed one after the other; sometimes she loved them, other times not. Nothing changed. The spell kept its hold. Frédérique had long ago decided to come to terms with it. After all, who else could boast of having a fail-safe way to achieve ecstasy? She kept her secret and contented herself with letting the pleasure take over without feeling shame or guilt any longer.

And then one day—she was then nearly thirty and living in London with her fiancé—she saw him in the street, walking just a few feet away from her. There was a woman on his arm, but not the German, who'd surely returned long ago to her beloved country. She looked at him, lingering on his aquiline nose, on his inimitable smile.

Suddenly, she understood what she had to do. Hadn't she become attractive enough, woman enough for that? And wouldn't that be the only way to free herself from the evil spell?

She began by heading cautiously in his direction, without him seeing her. She gave herself some time to prepare, to gather her strength, to summon all the confidence she'd gained over the past fifteen years.

She'd go up to him casually, talk about Martinique, about Raoul (the one who'd done well in life), about the house with the pool, Aunt Gilda's succulent dishes...about all of it. And he'd remember it all. Even the twins, even the one who was slightly grumpy, a bit of a tomboy, whom he wouldn't recognize in this graceful, self-assured Londoner.

She walked at a snail's pace. Looked at her reflection in a shop window. She adjusted her bearing, straightened her body to its full height—that body whose harmony she could now see. That body she would soon give over to him entirely.

"Well, if it isn't the little pianist herself, in person!" That's what he'd say, and he'd mention the Chopin waltz. Then, carried along by that flash of memory, he'd recall her name—he'd say her first name in a burst of laughter, which they would share. The woman on his arm would grimace, understanding well before he did what this girl, encountered by chance, was looking for.

Frédérique continued her slow advance, wiping her moist hands on her skirt, trying to tame the beating of her heart, pushing away, most importantly, the hypnosis of fifteen years ago. She pretended not to notice the diabolical current she already felt coming back to her thighs, her belly, at the mere sight of the Nigerian walking on the same sidewalk—a feeling that intensified with every step. She kept repeating to herself what she'd say to him.

All she would have to do was speak, and everything else would follow—with all due respect to his new companion—until the designated spot, an as-yet secret place that she'd know how to find, and where, in the broad light of day, eyes wide open this time, she would guide the actor in what was, unbeknownst to him, just one of their many embraces.

The couple turned onto a side street. Frédérique picked up her pace.

Yes, she'd do what she had to do. And then, she'd be free.

FABIENNE KANOR

Plato's
Stars

TRANSLATED BY LYNN E. PALERMO

Je prenais les commandes lorsque le silence a pété,
un silence comme un coup de fusil.

THERE, WHERE THE PAVEMENT FORKS, THAT'S WHERE HE hid. Or rather, tried his luck. They'd promised a car would come by to pick him up. He walked out to the crossroads and it started drizzling, but he stuck it out, staring stubbornly down the road. The rain was just bad luck. For weeks, it had been our albatross, pouring down endlessly and making Plato, the TV weatherman, jabber on. Every evening, at the end of the news, he forecast a return of the stars. Stars! But when daylight rolled around again, the wretched sky still wore its blasted, lead-gray, morning-after maw. It was so bad, I'd had to dig out my *popof* and resort to sheathing my feet in plastic. Me, in galoshes. I, who pride myself on my look and consider elegance a universal duty.

Monday dawned and, how can I say this, I don't know why, but when I smacked the blaring alarm clock, I had a feeling that something, something else besides the rain, was going to happen. On Monday it's always rush rush rush. I get moving to make Camille get moving; I bundle her up in her little-girl clothes, lace up her shoes, wrestle with the zipper on her anorak, and in the dismal morning under the street-lights, drive her to school, dropping her off right out front. That morning I didn't linger. I started the car right up again. To avoid the gang of mothers. Keep secret what they knew already: that my boss Lionel Beaufils might not keep me on. Three waitresses on the payroll is too many. Means he makes less money, then loses his temper over a trifle and yells at his wife.

He punched her. Or so I assumed that morning from his craven fists and his not-very-proud, blowhard stride. Shameful. But I played along. As if the jokes he muttered were the most hilarious I'd ever heard. As if he would always be the boss, no matter how pathetic he felt, and I, Arielle, could ask for nothing better than this brewery where I'd been grinding myself down for over six years now. Because money doesn't grow on trees.

In general, our regulars spill out of their offices for lunch around noon. I waited until a quarter to, then locked myself in the toilets to touch up my lipstick. I smile only when I'm wearing it. So it won't be wasted.

I was taking orders when a silence exploded, a silence like gunshot. The boss stopped joking around. Our customers and my coworkers sat stunned, their eyes glued to the giant who had just walked in and planted his elbows on the bar. Out of ease or exhaustion, he rolled up his soaked shirtsleeves, swore, excused himself with "I'm thirsty."

I filled his glass, checking out his arms. I don't know, I didn't notice his face. Only this: his sculpted hands and elegant arms, which reminded me of Dominique. I'd lasted three years with Dominique. He was an artist, but easily set off. One day, I told the police everything.

He was dehydrated, so I served him another glass. Looking back, maybe that's the moment when I picked up on the rest: the odor of travel under the sweater that gaped open; the scent, yes, the scent on his clothes; the brown paper envelope that served as change purse, wallet, shoulder bag; and the voice that pulled back from intensity, feigned cheerfulness to put people at ease, reassure. He wouldn't be staying long, he was passing through.

He came back. All week, at the same hour, he came back. He hardly spoke, never stayed long, drank sodas, and then sat over there, see? Just over there, behind the coatrack. By the second day, his presence was making people uncomfortable, but ultimately, they forgot about him. So long as he paid, so long as he bothered no one.

I said *a week*, but it didn't go on that long. I remember it was Thursday when I found him standing outside in front of my car. I looked around, but there was no one else in the parking lot. He was waiting for *me*. You can't evaluate people's real needs based on what they say. What I mean is, there are people who are champions at demanding what they already have, while others ask for nothing even when they are in need; there's no way to know, that would be too simple, it would be so much simpler if you could just give when you had to. With this sick sky, we couldn't stand there and chat, nobody could have, not even briefly, not even for just a sec, at the very least we'd have to take shelter in my car, hoping the rain would calm down—lord, what a torrent!—and get out of there, at the very least I'd drive him to the fork in the road where a car was supposed to pick him up. When? Darkness was falling. The road was treacherous at night.

"Is that your daughter?" he asked, pointing to the photo pendant hanging from the rearview mirror. "What's her name?" I spelled out her first name for him. I checked the time. There was no rush; Camille was sleeping over at Clémentine's house. Those two are best friends, they do their hair alike, eat alike, laugh alike; they swear that when they grow up they're going to trade husbands and all four of them, Clémentine, Camille, and the two husbands, are going to have children and raise them together. In the beginning, when we first came to this town, they hated each other. Camille pulled Clémentine's pigtails and Clémentine called Camille *picrone*, little mosquito. Then one day, they clicked. You couldn't pull them apart.

The road was bucking like the sea through the start and stop of the windshield wipers. "They're shorting out," my boss had told me the week before. He'd recommended anti-Regen spray to clear the raindrops accumulating on the windshield. It's German, you can buy it at Leclerc. I'm not exaggerating, there was no way to figure out what this road wanted, so much so that I turned left instead of right, completely missed the intersection, and then, to my surprise, found myself on the road leading to the house. I should have had the windshield wipers repaired, my mistake, an error of judgment, but like I said, it's not like we were being paid piecework or anything; we had all night.

It's also a matter of social status. When you're a single mother, being alone takes its toll: The solitude weighs on you. It drags you down and makes you paranoid. We start to believe that the problem lies with us, that if nobody whistles at us in the street or ogles our legs, our behind, it means we're not worth a red cent. At the same time, I cherish my peace of mind, and ever since my breakup with Dominique, I have become very watchful, suspicious. I waver between having some pain-in-the neck on my hands and having no kind of life at all. But I suppose that's how it is with everything: You have to find a happy medium.

My confusion made him laugh. He laughed and so did I. I laughed because if one of us was a lost soul, it sure wasn't me. This was my home. I knew the city, I paid taxes, insurance, rent, the school cafeteria. I had a job. And every month, I made another payment on my living-room furniture.

He said nothing as he walked into my house, no *This is pretty*, *Feels better in here*, or *This is a big place*. He sat down on the chair I offered him and just took off his shoes. Strange shoes for such a hefty man, too small by at least two sizes, gleaming yellow leather so shiny that I wondered how, and especially where, in the world he'd found the polish and time to shine these Bozo-the-clown shoes so poorly suited to travel, to the wet muddy nights I didn't want to know about. I'm scared of misfortune. And like everyone else, when I run into it, I don't try to understand, I scamper away. If things aren't going well, they're not going well. It has nothing to do with my competence.

I know what you're thinking, but even on that subject, there's nothing unusual or extraordinary to tell. He was consenting, I was okay with it; we did our thing. Much later, he was the one who started talking. I can't tell you where he was from, if that's what you're after. I don't know those lands. If he'd said *Dakar*, at least it would have meant something to me, especially now. Dakar, you hear about it sometimes; we all have a friend who's been there on vacation. But as for his country, honestly, the name escapes me; he could have been speaking

Chinese, for all I understood. I nodded so I wouldn't offend him. You have to be civil.

On the other hand, I remember hearing about the wife or mother he'd left behind, the one he would contact as soon as he found a safe place to stay. He kept saying she was a jewel—I heard "drool"—and I thought, if he were my Camille and I were his mother, I would be sad not knowing where my child was living, I would want him to call me; it's silly, but I couldn't stop thinking about that as he described her face in a thick voice, not forced like his voice at the bar, but as if he had all eternity in his mouth. I'll have to call that lady one of these days to tell her what happened; a woman needs to know what's happened to her son or her husband. I'll have to do it; after all, that's our duty too.

I took him into my house; an innkeeper could have done no better. I offered him a drink, a place to sleep, hospitality, my own food, and not just any food: fresh meat with all its *couenne*, as well as a salad bowl full of pasta, the way my father's father made it. He's the one who showed me how to cook it to keep it a little crunchy. He used to say, above all, the key to pasta is its sound. When you hear *couic*, dinner's ready!

That evening on TV, Plato surrendered to the might of the Heavens, his face tight. He acknowledged that this endless rain was a first in our region, and if the situation continued, schools would be closed, rooms opened up in the hospital, vulnerable people evacuated. All residents would be protected. They would do what had been done in Louisiana during the disaster: They would pack the needy into the municipal stadium until the sky dried out. The newscaster agreed with Plato's assessment, and so did the singer who'd been invited on the show. Everyone seemed in agreement and involved.

The evening film started. I watched the beginning then went up to my bedroom alone. Because water seemed to have bored into his lungs and the car had not come past, he couldn't sleep. Through my locked bedroom door, I could hear him cough, getup-sitdown on the sofa. At last, he dozed off and I did the same, my telephone within reach.

I'm not responsible for the rest. Of course, I was uncomfortable seeing this man in my living room again the next morning, this man who meant nothing to me, but what could I do? I couldn't throw him out, make coffee right under his nose and not offer him a cup; I couldn't yell *Out with you!* and tell him to gather up his bag, his secondhand clothes that were still depressing, despite two hours of disinfecting, despite fabric softener. There are some lines you just don't cross as a human being, especially as a woman alone and defenseless.

I gave him soap, a toothbrush, new socks, a clean shirt, and the end of a bottle of eau de cologne that I had. I kind of like jasmine. I apply a few drops under my arms before going to work. Makes the customers happy when I walk past their table. It smells fresh and lasts a long time.

I suggested taking him back to La Fourche. Exactly where in La Fourche, I didn't know, but in any case, it was better than making him set out on foot, especially in this rain. Because my shift started at noon, I pulled over onto the shoulder to put on makeup. No, he didn't touch me. He never took his eyes off the pavement. He really seemed to believe his story, that this car, a maroon van, apparently, was no fairytale, that it really drove past from time to time, picking up guys like him and taking them far from here to somewhere safe. Maybe even took them home. Who knows? I don't want to know.

He got out of the car. It was raining so hard that I couldn't make out his words through the window. He must have said something like *Thanks so much I won't forget what you've done*, because, right after, in a sign of gratitude, he turned back toward me and put his hand on his heart, which wasn't actually his heart, but the pocket on the jacket that I had carefully ironed, so he would look clean, like someone you might call *monsieur*, someone you might stop for without fear, when you saw him standing at the edge of town, his thumb stuck out toward the sign reading "Other Directions." As I pulled away, a vehicle coming toward me honked. I braked, ready to stop, but the vehicle sped past. It wasn't a van. I thought *that's too bad*, and continued on to the Beaufils parking lot, which used to be called the Pablo Neruda parking lot before somebody tore the sign down.

I hadn't even slipped on my apron before the boss was raising his voice at me. He scolded me for being late and for errors calculating my drawer. It was all nonsense, but I didn't deny anything. I knocked on wood; I did not want to be fired. As I'd expected, he refused to let me leave early to pick up Camille. I had to warn Sandrine, Clémentine's mama, that I'd hit a snag. Sandrine was accommodating, but I was upset for Camille. Friday is our special day. We go to the movies and eat popcorn. We sit in the back row and laugh out loud on purpose. The two of us.

Finally, it was time: I closed out the cash register, went down to the toilets, and pulled my galoshes back on. In the mirror, I looked snuffed out; there was nothing left of the night before. With Dominique, my body had moved like a spark. When I left his hands, I smelled like wood.

I splashed water on my face, thinking about the giant's song, the one that he'd carried with him and sung in my bathroom. Like a soldier performing an anthem, he articulated the words properly. He had learned them when he was Camille's age. Over there in his country at the Brothers' school, they were spanked when they got tangled up in the verses.

It's curious, but with time, my memory grows sharper, details come back to me.

They didn't know that they weren't alone in the brewery and that I could hear them. Otherwise, they wouldn't have had so much to drink, they wouldn't have dared to soil my name, for it was directed at me, Arielle-the-harlot, the hussy, the tramp! and so on; obviously my boss, his brother-in-law, and their two good friends were full of insults. I didn't catch everything they said, but god, how I burned with shame at that moment, how I wished the rain would swallow me right up or else cleanse me of a sin that must be real, since it made them rabid, since it kept these men alert and upright, men who were completely drunk, on the verge of rolling under the table. If I hadn't been such a chicken, I would have stormed out of the toilets to confront them directly. Let them correct me, like they did Beaufils' wife every night when her husband counted the money. Let them immolate me in the Neruda parking lot. The big reporters from the local television station that employed Plato would love that.

But I am not brave. I did not come out of my hideout until after the men had left.

How they were going to spend their night was not even on my mind. Our old town is so small. We don't have many places where a man who has been drinking can keep drinking and blow off a little steam. Apart from Saturday, there's not much carousing.

We are a cautious, sheltered community. But we were once young, proud: We walked with long strides too, and we were welcomed, we were served like I serve my boss's customers, with the same dedication, the same innocence. We believed in the world.

Please excuse the digression, I'm so tired.

At last, the rain tapered off, the road took on its contours, and the windshield wipers worked again. The night was now a blessing. Coming into La Fourche, I had to stop to be sure that what I thought I'd seen really was what my eyes were seeing. Not a wild animal, no, hardly any of those around anymore. It was several men who had knelt down and were now lifting a sausage-like package wrapped in a white canvas tarp. I didn't *stop*, exactly, more like slowed down, as the procession drifted toward the big tree marking the entrance to La Fourche. From inside the car, I heard them laugh, curse their prize catch, spit on it. They were kicking a big clown shoe like a soccer ball.

No.

Yes.

I put my foot on the gas. I knew that night is a trap and my little one was waiting for me at Sandrine's house.

Marie-Célie Agnant

Incandescences
*
Inventory
*
O My Land
*
Fervent Prayer

Translated by Danielle Legros Georges

Dans ma tête et dans mes veines
cette musique

Incandescences

In the corridors of my memory
in the bundle of broken keepsakes
roams
daïva
hustler
depending on the day
a man so hungry
he becomes a bull
hips lifting and falling
to the rhythm of rage
feet merging with asphalt
memories
the smell of liquor
rotten mangoes
the sellers of bottles
trinkets
stuff
toothless Marias crumbling under filth
courtyard of miracles
shit-drains

cradle of black children
rancid fried food
refried
in the sun
and this echo of flies
of bees
of acid laughter
bonbon sirop
gingerbread
sewer spitting up its stench
in the corridors of my memory
abrupt recollections
desperate
prickly
dizzying
procession of mummies
symphony of anxieties
sweatbaths
mud

Inventory

Flower Flame Woman Fountain
they wanted you vestal
they wanted you flame
flame-vestal woman-fortress
to watch over
to comfort
to give life
with fragile sexes
frigid

They wanted you vestal-flame-woman
woman-fortress woman-navel
woman thrusting
delicate flower
engulfed by the transient waves
of attraction's seasons

They wanted you river they wanted you crystal
crystal-fountain
clear and mute river

troubling
giving intoxicating
cave of Alibaba
they wanted you flame-woman-flower
crystal-fountain
vestal-amazon
infibulated open

They wanted you ocean
cave stream
site of confused desires
gone astray
awkward chained
forever
wanting
mute guilty

Woman with no luggage
with no memories of your own dreams, you go
stumbling across your part of the world
you go
I write to celebrate
your body of indulgence
sketched by my often-clumsy lips

your sex hungry for new breath
to express
your best seasons
long cut away

O My Land

You held the joy
of all my springs hostage
my voice captive
in that season
of whispers
I kept within me O my land
memories of your worried entrails
your voice this muffled flute

I kept the memory of the fear that besieged your walls
and the stubborn magic
of that time despite every shock

I recall
how the stars shot across the sky
yet beneath your false eyelashes and kohl
there, your weary gaze
facing time's dirty windows

Back then

we chased, you and I,
a pyromaniac wind
that would destroy
this saying

And in our temples in long streaks of fire
raged our dizzy dreams
our fire-red birthdays

So many stars shot across the night skies
yet our silhouettes
black and pitiful
joined the shadows of the barbed wire
raised against the favelas in our piece of America
It was Bogota Port-au-Prince or Rio
where all the windows of life
had that shade, dirty, stubborn
had days long as years

Through hurricanes and storms
you and I
so often
saw life rise and die

Then in the hold in that haunting
of a miracle
I bequeathed my scales to your ocean
to become
from starboard to port
a piece of land without a will

I kept the image of your face
strangled by silence O my land
with so much cursed sperm
spilled on you
with so many men leaving
their footprints on your bed
and here the sea itself
day after day persists in betraying you

with no more
port for your dreams

Fervent Prayer

Stamped in my memory, faithfully
the countryside bearing the scent of burnt cane
breath and caress of the wind on my eyelids
the meadow's saffron
dandelion...
no need to know your name
fruit so sweet and fragrant
gifts from heaven
whose kisses we peel into our mouths

Memories
string of pearls
of dust
dangling in the warm air
beneath the table at dusk
a cat sleeping innocently
eyes blinking

And outside everything changing
leaving only the taste

as after love
the contours
all else fading

In my head, in my veins, this music
pleasure and sadness
oracles of the drum
coming down the mountain

This muffled music
carrying such strange quivers
down the spine
and already outside
the metal night
the blood cascading through the rills

MARIE-CÉLIE AGNANT

The Last Photograph

TRANSLATED BY DAWN FULTON

Je pensais, parfois, en entendant
   les gens avoir recours à cet euphémisme,
      lorsque à mots couverts ils parlaient
   de toi, aux oiseaux qui s'enfuient,
aux navires, engloutis par les tourbillons
     marins, aux étoiles qui s'éteignent.

For Rose-Flore and Carine Bélizaire

HOW COULD IT BE THAT I WOULD HAVE TO SPEND THE REST of my life without you? My first seven years moored around you. You bought me a red and yellow bicycle—my first bike— for my birthday. Just a few days later, you were gone. My love for that bike drained away too. I started waiting for you to come back, and time and absence became one. It's been more than forty years now, but from the beginning, when we lost you, I understood that for us—my sisters and my older brother—this sadness would have nothing to do with weeks or months, even less with years. When you left, time became an ache that still pierces me to the bone.

Time and the hole you left behind that we've come to call, carefully, your "passing." As if a father can simply pass to nowhere. When people spoke of you in their hushed tones, I'd think of birds flying off, of ships engulfed by ocean swells, of stars going out.

The years did not stop. But I stayed frozen within them without a name to give to your absence. I could not say out loud that you, like so many others, had been abducted, assassinated: not a passing but a crime, a killing by contract. Until I was ten, I would lower my head and say, "Papa's not here." But someone who is not here has to come back one day. So I learned to avert my eyes instead, to keep the lie and the pity at bay.

People think children's memories are made of garlands and colorful candies. But mine spread through me like dark tendrils, bitter strands that wind tighter and tighter, entangling me. The cadence of birthdays, the rituals of New Year's and Easter, our summer vacation trips, the things that marked out the rhythm of life, of our lives with you, all lost their magic. After your passing that June, we stopped celebrating. This ache, this time frozen in loss and pain, became our daily routine, darkening everything in its path like a fire. As the days and years went by, always the gnawing doubt: "Will my father come home tonight? Maybe that car in the distance is him..." I spent whole nights bartering your return with a silent God. "That man, who seems to be looking for something—please, merciful God, please let it be him. Dear Lord, if he comes back, I promise you, I will take the oath of priesthood and become your servant forever."

It was in June that everything fell apart, the year I turned seven. Gentle June, leaving the full glory of summer to July, still has days that burst open and flood the sky. I remember the light, clear and calm, so soft that everything felt wrapped in tenderness. And so, that final morning, seeing us all clustered around our mother on the stoop, you got out of the car and went back into the house, scaling the stairs to your office. Mama was smiling, and we were flocked all around her like sparrows. You handed her the camera. "Me and my children," you laughed. Your voice is still in my ears, after all this time. Mama laughed back, put her hands on her hips, and asked if the children belonged just to you.

That photo of you, with us. Your last photograph. Your one arm around my shoulders, the other holding Pedro's hand, and our sisters beside us: Lou gazing at you as usual, so that you can only see her profile, and Jena sulking about something.

Slowly the car rolled toward the gate and onto the dusty road. We stayed a few moments on the stairs, Lou in tears. She was only five.

More than forty years. My hair is gray and I miss my father.

Sometimes, in sleep, the crunch of gravel under tires comes back to me, the sharp clang of the iron gate closing. And your face. You seemed happy that day. On your way to Mérottes to get the house ready for our vacation. This comes back to me, and so many other things, but never you.

To piece the memory back together, I'd have to find the key, the one that would bring me to where the shards are scattered, so I could begin to gather them back up. Instead, I'm retracing my steps over and over, and all I have is the stubborn silence of everyone around me, and the insistent echo of a voice, thick with grief. My mother's voice: "There's no use, little one..." Her voice trembling. "No use in going on." The sighs of pain that punctuated her words reverberate inside me like a gong or the distress call of a sinking ship. Beginning that June day, Mama did start to sink. She broke inside, held upright only by the force of necessity, it seemed, because we were there—four mouths to feed, four children to raise.

Time slipped by, each day drawing the hope of seeing you a little further away. And then there was the house where you were headed, where we were coming to join you. That country house had been your studio and your sanctuary. You came alive when you were there. With its spiked cornices it looked like a bird floating on the water, gazing down at its reflection with its wings outstretched. You called it "pretty girl" sometimes, but its real name was the Blue Pigeon. That was the name your grandfather had given it. He was the one who'd built it up on the hill overlooking the water, and given it its indigo dress, adding a crown of sky-blue wooden lace-work around the gables and the edges of the roof. Did you reach the house that day? Or had your assassins, unleashed like vultures, descended upon you before you got there? No one has ever been able to tell us what really happened. You became a missing person, a father disappeared, evaporated like a cloud.

Your brothers and sisters, along with some of Mama's friends and relatives, went through everything in the house. But even with the bright sunlight splashing through the windows, they found nothing. The house a dark desert now, cold and empty. In your studio, unfinished sculptures waiting for you like wounded soldiers on a battlefield.

And below the house, that stretch of still water. Silent, only the slightest of ripples here and there, impassive and unchanging.

Was it a pond, a lake? Hard to know at seven. We'd decided to call it a river. The house stood facing it, and because it kept so quiet and still, I began to think of it as an accomplice. Its uneasy silence began to torment me. For a long time, I thought it might hold some clue to your disappearance.

Like everything from that time, that stretch of water is always with me, a ghost haunting every corner of my home, every part of my brain. For years I was sure that you had to be at the bottom of that silent water, that your killers had thrown your body in there. My head filled with fantastical tales of Maman Dlo, bewitching sirens, and maneaters, I imagined that all the evil haunting our waters had gotten hold of you. I made up so many stories of seeing you standing on the shore before being pulled down by some creature who'd trapped you in its hair and dragged you under the water, its skin shining in the moonlight. Almost everything having to do with your disappearance had happened when you were in that house or on the way there. The key, I would insist to Mama, had to be in that water.

For a long time afterward, in the house and even out in the garden, there was the heady smell of light tobacco, the kind you'd liked. At first it would be faint and subtle, barely a hint. Then, suddenly, there'd be thick blue rings dissolving into a white swirl. I was the only one guilty of seeing those swirls of smoke, until one day, alarmed by my delusions, Mama made the heartbreaking decision to part with the Blue Pigeon. I still have the briar pipe that I found in your studio. There's still a smell of light tobacco in the air around me.

So many Junes have passed since then, so many tears shed by the river, on the front steps of the house, and in the unkempt garden that even the wild turkeys had abandoned. The first few years, I'd cry out my despair to the trees and to the reeds that danced on the water's edge. But there was no response. Nothing came to enlighten or console us. No path through the mystery.

Then, one night, a man showed up looking for Mama. He was bony, like sticks of pine. Bristling eyebrows, a terse voice, and his eyes bulging marbles in his icy face. He stood there as we huddled around our mother's skirts and said: "These are the keys to your husband's car, do you recognize them? The papers are in the glove box. You know what the car is worth, give me the money and it's yours!"

He was well known, a member of Satrapier's inner circle, you told us years later. Sycophant, hatchet man, torturer, he had a long record in the regime. And you, Mama, you asked him if he would please repeat what he'd said. We drew in close around you. The panic we'd seen flicker across your face was gone, as you pointed slowly and deliberately at the door, screaming at him with all your strength: "Get out! Get out of this house!" The words burst out of you with a rage you did your best to contain. Despite the years of waiting and searching, you still had your dignity. You'd hung onto what was left of your strength, to keep on living...one day at a time, you kept saying, even if we didn't always understand. So often you'd start crying and beg us for forgiveness. "Forgive me," you'd say over and over, pulling us close as we trembled against you, "Forgive me for losing hold of myself. I don't know how to be anyone anymore—least of all your mother, since I can't protect you from hate or pain."

Even as a seven-year-old child, I understood instinctively that an unspoken rule, a kind of collusion, binds us all together here. That's why I could never talk about your disappearance with my friends at school, Papa. But I knew that they knew. Everyone knew, they all whispered about it. "Poor kids, their father's gone," the kinder parents would murmur behind my back, with a nod, a furtive glance. Oh... How sad! they might sigh. Some days, like a puppy starved for affection, I would go bask in the fatherly warmth of my friends, then return home to bury my head in my pillow and cry.

You were the father, our father, our mainstay, the center of everything. That's how the four of us felt and how I think we still feel. But all the tenderness you can see in that photo, the tenderness in your arms, in your sparkling eyes, the tenderness that demanded that last photograph with us, all that and everything else is scattered and gone. Now we make copies of the photograph so that we can pass it on, like a relic, to our children. We give it to them in the vain attempt to name what can't be named: your absence.

We've come to say your name like a prayer in the silence of night. That's how I call you, how I talk to you, when I can't sleep. My hair is getting thin and my steps are beginning to falter, and yet I plead with you, senselessly, over and over, to hear me, to come back, to end this absence.

Another thing I knew at age seven was that in order to live I would have to erase your very existence from my memory. So I already understood that I was dying. A little every day, dying from your absence, from not having you there. These images that I revisit hopelessly day and night are a poison seeping into my veins, drowning me. They come in waves, always the same. They come rushing at me, grasping; they seethe inside me, leaving me weak, trembling and mute with a helpless anger, my eyes fixed on your photograph, always that photograph, your last photograph.

KETTLY MARS

from
The Patriarch's
Angel

TRANSLATED BY LUCY SCOTT

Edwin et Vanika ne font qu'un sur la moto.

EDWIN AND VANIKA ARE AS ONE ON THE BACK OF THE
motorcycle. The wind lashes at them, and they shiver in their
lightweight clothes. Edwin's never had such a crazy night in his
entire life. He doesn't know whose house that was, but it's clear
that he and Vanika won't ever be setting foot in there again. It's
not like he has the money to treat himself to bougie parties.
A friend of a friend at school had told him that there would be
drinks and good eats for anyone stopping by house X on Friday
night. He'd written down the address to Montagne Noire, telling
himself that he should live it up at least once in his life.

A few dozen cars were already parked along the street when
they'd arrived a few hours earlier. Edwin didn't have any trou-
ble finding the house. A white villa with a neo-antique façade,
a long driveway lined on both sides with turfgrass, some
bougainvillea, blossoming frangipani trees, a veritable floral
frenzy. The guard showed him where to park his bike inside the
gate. The party was in the west wing of the villa, in a room two
stories tall with windows flanked by floor-length silk drapes

of white openwork lace. Sculptures and large vases filled with fresh flowers were placed tastefully throughout the space. A spotlight illuminated a superb Burton Chenet mural at second-story level on the back wall. The view of the vibrant fauna was striking from all angles. No one had asked them for anything at the door, not their names, not their parents' names, not their bank account information. Admission to the party was totally free. Edwin breathed a sigh of relief. He was trying to play it cool, but underneath his aloof exterior, he'd been worried that someone would stop him from entering this Eden.

At the start of the party, Vanika and Edwin felt out of place among so many strange faces. There were scions from wealthy families along with a small number of outsiders—young drifters like them without prominent surnames or fancy backgrounds who'd stumbled into the party by chance. It didn't matter that they'd dressed as nicely as they could in Nike or Hugo Boss; in a place this upscale, money or lack of it was apparent at a glance. Not once that whole night did Edwin see the friend of a friend who'd given him the head's up about the party. One glass of wine down and he and Vanika were blending into the environment. The bar was fully stocked, the servers generous and discreet. In the corner of the great hall was a catered buffet, with all the mini sandwiches and scrumptious hors d'oeuvres they could ever want there for the taking.

As it started to rain, the atmosphere took an enchanting turn, droplets of rain adorning the trees and lawn, resembling diamond dust in the garden's subdued lighting. The DJ was in a trance, playing a continuous mix of the latest Caribbean, American, and Latin hits to an electrified crowd. Jam-packed together, the partygoers erupted in cries of pleasure each time the voices of their favorite showbiz demigods played over the speakers, each time the booming bass caused the music to reverberate through their guts and loins. Every now and then someone would lift an arm and the camera flash from their smartphone would capture their smiling, sweaty bodies in photos they then posted to social media in real time. Some of the revelers snuck out to the garden to smoke joints in small groups behind the fan of a traveler's palm tree. Edwin would lose sight of Vanika and then bump into her again. They'd nudge each other and smile, still a bit incredulous in the face of so much euphoria. And then they'd head back out separately to dance with someone else. They weren't too worried about being apart; they'd just end up finding each other again. Most of the girls at the party were drinking too much and didn't need any persuading to roll their hips and shake their asses with two or three dance partners.

Edwin drank, ate, and danced. Inhibitions loosened by the alcohol, he made out with the girls who were game for it, pretty girls he wouldn't meet again and who wouldn't even recognize him once the party was over. He knew he was drinking too much, but the life he was living in this moment was so good, so strong. He was discovering that life could be magnificent, like a dream, even if it was someone else's dream. Vanika was gorgeous, her skin midnight black, her lips plump, her nostrils wide, dimples cutting deep when she smiled. Her eyes shone like two small moons. Her body aroused fantasies in men and women. Plenty of boys had noticed her and were taking turns dancing with her, breathing in her smell. They wanted to know where she was from, who she was. She wasn't from their world, and the mystery of her was excruciatingly attractive. Sipping cocktails, Vanika smiled sweetly, brushing aside their questions. She and Edwin left the party with the last group to go home. They had drunk down the night to the very last drop. They didn't say good night to anyone else and went back to being as anonymous as when they'd come in.

Edwin and Vanika are as one on the back of the motorcycle. The hills of Montagne Noire are steep and dangerous to drive down once it rains. Their brains are still foggy, intoxicated by alcohol and pure glee. The beat of the music is still drumming in their ears, mixing with the backfire from the motorcycle. Edwin has a death grip on the handlebars to stay on the road. Under his helmet, his eyelids are heavy. He concentrates on not losing control of the bike. The engine seems to take on a life of its own, refusing to follow his commands. Vanika clings tightly to Edwin so as not to give in to the crazy desire to throw herself into the abyss, arms open wide, head thrown back, eyes lost to the expanse of the sky. She wants to laugh and never stop laughing. To laugh or die. They drive along Boyer Plaza, deserted at this hour, no police patrols; even the hookers have gone home. They cut across the intersection at the old cemetery in Pétion-Ville, still waiting to be turned into a bus station, and then soar down the road toward Frères. It's virtually a straight shot to Pernier, just three or four miles, and they're speeding along in a daze. Finally, they make it back home. Edwin parks his bike under the carport, Vanika hopping unsteadily off the bike in her high heels. They live in a modest two-bedroom apartment in a corner of Pernier past where the paved roads end. The dense clouds draping over the night part to reveal a sliver of the full moon, a strangely beautiful light melding into the break of dawn. They each have a bedroom to themselves and share one larger room that combines kitchen, dining room, and living room. The tiny bathroom between their bedrooms can hardly fit two people at a time and smells faintly of urine. Running water is a luxury in this area. They return to their rooms without saying another word to each other, completely wiped out, the alcohol lowering their blood oxygen levels.

Edwin kicks off his shoes, his jeans, keeps on his shirt, and collapses into bed.

As if through a fog, he hears the door to his room open. Vanika has come to find him. Barefoot on the green mosaic tiles, she's wearing a blue T-shirt and orange panties. She slides into bed with him.

"I'm cold, can I stay with you for a bit?"

"Yeah... If you want."

He says this as he turns over to fall asleep. They're both quiet. It's a calm night; the dogs have stopped barking. A cautious crowing rooster greets the coolness of dawn. Vanika sighs and snuggles against Edwin's back. He shifts to put space between them, but she snuggles closer. As he drifts off to sleep, the alcohol crashes against his head like a wave, and he feels himself sinking into a hole. Vanika's warmth at his back keeps him from falling off the precipice. He's happy she's there. Her hand tethers him to solid ground, the hand that she's now sliding under his shirt. He lets out a sigh. She teases his nipple. His anesthetized brain doesn't react. She breathes more heavily; he feels her warm breath on the back of his neck. She shoves her nose into his armpit to breathe him in, to smell him; he hasn't showered off all the sweat from the party yet. She closes her eyes and sighs. Edwin can feel himself getting hard. He tells himself it's time for her to go back to her room. The idea hovers for a second, passes before his closed eyes, and disappears. Vanika lowers her hand, her fingers tracing the muscles on his stomach, the edge of his pelvis. Edwin tries to pull himself out of his stupor. But his will is as soft as jelly. Vanika strokes him more firmly, producing the effect she wanted. She finally wraps her warm hand around his hard member, planning to take him to paradise. Edwin is suffocating. He can't get enough air. Vanika isn't letting him breathe. I need air, quick! He jumps out of bed, gasping, his lungs at the point of exploding. In disbelief, he looks at Vanika, still lying in bed. She's also looking at him, motions him back to bed. He doesn't recognize her eyes. Edwin has trouble finding words to speak. She's staring at the bulge in his drawers. She breathes out:

"You want me too, Edwin. Look at the state you're in…"

Edwin shuts his eyes, opens them again, waiting for the scene to change. Maybe he just hasn't sobered up yet. But no, he's still in the same panic-inducing situation. Vanika stands up and hugs him. She seeks his lips. He snaps his head away, violently shoving her away from him. She falls down on her butt onto the bed. He takes advantage of the moment to quickly grab his jeans from a nearby chair and pull them on.

"What are you doing, Edwin? You're going to just leave me like this, all hot and bothered?"

Edwin leaves the room. Vanika follows him, her fists opening and closing, breathing through her mouth. Edwin understands that there isn't any possible dialogue for this surreal piece of theater. A few burning seconds go by. Then she's back on the attack, trying to pin him against the dining table.

"What do they have that I don't, all those stupid bougie bitches you were groping all night?"

Edwin grabs her wrists and holds them hard enough to break. He looks her straight in the eye and says slowly, pausing after each word:

"They're. Not. My. Sisters."

Vanika's enjoying the pain Edwin's causing her. She doesn't seem to have heard his response. When she next speaks, her voice is so hoarse it's unrecognizable.

"Make love to me. Just the one time. Just once!"

Edwin feels like crying. He turns to Vanika, nearly pleading:

"I'm not some dirty old goat chasing after my own sister's tail, Vanika! What's up with you, for the love of God!"

"Leave God out of it, Edwin. Get your ass over here."

Edwin's tired. He doesn't feel like fighting with Vanika. She's hysterical. Or maybe it's all the booze she drank; she'd never been out drinking this hard before. Maybe they drugged her at the party, who knows? It's like their night out is plastered to their skin. He shoves Vanika aside and runs to lock himself in the bathroom. She knocks on the door, yelling at him. "You dumb ass! You don't get it, do you? Are you a faggot? You'd rather screw guys? You'd rather be with those dirty rich bitches? Go fuck yourself! Limp-dick bastard! You don't know what you're missing out on. Fucking fairy! So fucking nasty!"

Vanika goes on hurling insults at Edwin for a few minutes. Then, tired, voice reduced to a croak, she goes back to her room, slamming the door shut. Edwin remains locked in the small bathroom and ends up dozing off right there on the toilet, his head resting on the wall behind him. Two or three hours later, when he emerges from the bathroom, it's broad daylight and the reassuring smell of coffee is floating through the house. The sunlight hurts his eyes. His entire body feels stiff. Vanika's sitting at her usual place at the dining room table. She's put on pants and a blouse, and she's drinking a large cup of coffee. She's recovered from last night and appears very calm.

"There's coffee on the stove," she says to him, just as she does every morning. Edwin goes and grabs himself a cup, the sweetened coffee burning his lips but doing him a world of good. Still cautious, he approaches Vanika, searching for the right words to say.

"Do you... Do you remember what happened last night?"

She looks at him, half smiling. "Of course, I remember."

*

The cars have been gridlocked for at least fifteen minutes. A mechanical capharnaum discharging a cocktail of black, gray, and blue smoke that seeps into the nostrils and sticks to the skin. To cross the street, pedestrians, students, and street vendors sidle between vehicles and motorcycles vibrant with heat. Exasperated honks erupt from cars every so often. Each intersection is blocked by stubborn drivers who don't want to back up a few feet to break the stalemate at their point in the traffic jam. Some traffic cops drenched in sweat roam the street, speaking into their walkie-talkies, but they don't manage to curb the density of the traffic jam. Edwin is at war with the hurried, aggressive motorcycle taxis riding up on the sidewalk to cut through traffic quicker. He steers between cars on John Brown Avenue. The sun hits his helmet. A midday sun that inexplicably appears in his line of sight no matter the direction he takes. A few days ago, his motorcycle started pulling to the right, which makes driving harder, more physical. His right shoulder hurts when he goes home tired to Pernier at the end of the day. He'll get the alignment checked next week. Edwin can't wait to be done with his classes. He needs to get to the bank, eat lunch, and go to his afternoon college classes. As he does at the end of every month, he stopped by the office of his uncle, Jules Carmel Jean-François, Esq., who gave him a check to cover their living expenses, Vanika's and his. The atmosphere at the firm Jean-François and Associates always has the same effect on him, the sense of entering a privileged place where intelligence and reason can untangle the twisted strands of human folly. Reverent, he caresses the large tomes on civil and penal law lining the shelves behind his uncle's desk. He loves to breathe in their odor and wonder at their precision in balancing emotions, feelings, laws, and duties. Imposing the force of Law. There's always someone waiting in the reception room, in front of the secretary's desk. Men or women fighting divorces until the bitter end, victims of the national sport of arbitrarily seizing land or property, evicted tenants who come anxiously in search of aid, a miniature humanity in dire straits waiting for men and women in judicial gowns to give a response to their anguish or a satisfaction to their bitterness. Edwin studies law. He wants to be a lawyer like his uncle, the man who's cared for him since the death of Isabelle, his half-sister. Among these waiting clients, perhaps there are illegitimate sons or daughters wishing to be acknowledged by their indelicate parents, today's science providing irrefutable paternity tests. Edwin might be one of them someday, but he'll serve as his own defense, he'll have the knowledge and the weapons to compel the man whose genes he carries to accept him, or at least admit he's his legitimate son. He won't do it for the money or for the benefits, but to set an example, because it's time for men to shoulder their responsibilities in this society or stop getting women pregnant whenever they please only to turn their backs on them, free of any burdens. Edwin is at the age of deep feelings and big dreams; he'd like to erase every injustice in the world, clad in his lawyer's robe. He's on good terms with his uncle, a man stern in nature and discreet in affections, and grateful for being taken under his wing following the death of his mother. They haven't talked about it, but Edwin aims to become an intern at the office of Jean-François once he finishes his studies. His uncle is satisfied with his diligence to his schoolwork and with his progress in general. It's the only condition he asked of his sister, struck down by cancer, on her death bed. He'd take care of the two children as long as they persevered with their studies. Edwin is the result of a complicated past like so many of this country's young people. He's the son of a political figure who had a fling with his mother, a pretty young woman from Miragoâne making a living as a hairdresser in a beauty salon. When Isabelle told him about her pregnancy, he adamantly refused paternity, and she never saw him again. The story of his younger sister, Vanika, is a different one. Isabelle never wanted to say who her father was, though he appeared to have been the great love of her life. Evidently, she hadn't been the great love of his. Her lover had insisted on an abortion, had given her the money for it, and had demanded this as the term for continuing their relationship, but she'd refused. They broke up over it. A proud woman, Isabelle couldn't get over her disappointment and never allowed that man to set foot through her door or even meet his child. Jules Carmel Jean-François, Esq., kept his promise. Edwin and Vanika, young adolescents, were placed in a boarding school, their tuition paid for. When Edwin came of age, the lawyer found them a house where they'd have a little more independence and learn to take care of themselves. When Edwin passed his entrance exam for law school, his uncle offered him a motorcycle to ease his commute and ensure his punctuality to classes.

Vanika didn't try to persuade Edwin to get up close and personal again, but their two bodies are under constant observation. The past is forgotten, repressed, in fact. Life has returned to its usual course in the small house in Pernier. Edwin goes to law school each day; Vanika takes her computer courses at the technical institute. Their friends come to their house to play cards and joke around. They haven't revisited that infamous night of outright craziness, of pure intoxication when they could've committed the irreparable. Nevertheless, an uneasiness is always there, wrapped in silence. Vanika, his cherished baby sister, is the same as ever, but a distance has settled between them. A painful distance. A veil covers Vanika's eyes, and he can no longer dive into them like before, immersing himself in her through waves of laughter, making fun of everything like they love doing so much. There's a shadow behind their joys now, a heaviness to their gestures. Edwin is unable to speak of that evening again. Vanika doesn't seem concerned about it. He would give anything to return to the time before that night in Montagne Noire, before that notorious party that, he felt, had resulted in the devil creeping into their lives.

After more than an hour in line at the bank, Edwin manages to deposit his check into his account and withdraw some cash. He then leaves John Brown Avenue, the sun always before his eyes, following him relentlessly. He thinks back to his plan to move closer to the law school and the college where Vanika studies. Pernier is a quiet place, and the rent there is affordable, but the daily commute is grueling. Edwin heads to Champ de Mars Plaza, where traffic is smoother and the streets wider. He drives past the national palace and turns left onto Oswald Durand Street. Despite his helmet, he feels as if the sun is boiling his gray matter in a water bath. He'll still have time to grab a bite to eat at a small restaurant that's popular among local students and relax a bit before classes. A funny odor rises out of his motorcycle's exhaust pipe. Edwin breathes in small, careful breaths. It's a smell like flesh burning. A faint white smoke surrounds him. The road is practically empty; he only sees a single car a dozen yards ahead and some pedestrians. He glances back to see if this sickening odor is coming from another car or from a battery in a trash heap burning on the curb. When he turns his head, it's as if he's already dead. His eyes only graze a silhouette arising on his right, and life stands still. He brakes a second too late at the edge of a sinkhole. The motorcycle skids, makes an astonishing leap forward, and goes sliding beneath the enormous wheels of a tank truck barreling toward him from the other direction.

ADLYNE BONHOMME

"I wait by the sea…"
*
"Here I am, a wound hanging…"
*
"We built the night…"
*
"Your naked tongue…"
*
"I approached the sand…"
*
"From our arms on the first
day of spring…"

TRANSLATED BY NATHAN H. DIZE

*Me voici geste
dans le vide*

I wait by the sea
Seated upright with
Autumn in my hand
I gather your sweat in creeper vines
fresh rain on the sidewalks
Muddled with a silence woven in those first nights
those first gestures
those first stones

Here I am, a wound hanging
in the window of your body
Etched on your moon
Wrapped up in your gaze
Fresh like your kiss on my tongue

Here I am, a gesture in the void
I am the city
Braided with cries of doubt
Here I am, dreams and bitter sunshine
Tell me today's story
in the language of ashes

We built the night
with a mauve kiss
flowering
on our vacationing lips
on our fluttering caresses
timid in the breeze
We constructed
our cathedral on a foundation of sweat

Your naked tongue
I am a thousand leaves
blended with folly
in the palm of a glass
Your naked tongue
a ripening scent
amid the secret of a flower
glistening with winter
Your naked tongue
my burning body
that I offer to the silence of the sea

I approached the sand
body in hand
Words blending with the sound of your steps
I kneel down
thousands of frozen movements in your tracks
and I draw your figure
with a petal of fleeting water

From our arms on the first day of spring
to our thoughts composed of ink
Everywhere needs walls streets pavers
To write this silence
in water's hand
in the afternoon by the sea
in the nudity of the hour

Suzanne Dracius

The Macho's Marathon, the Major's Martyrology, and the Coqueur's Calvary

Translated by Nancy Naomi Carlson
and Catherine Maigret Kellogg

*Grand pêcheur devant l'Éternel et fier de
l'être, le voilà pris dans la nasse,
piégé dans son réseau de bonnes femmes
qu'il a lui-même organisé.*

Translators' Note: *Nègzagonale* is a pejorative term used to describe a woman
born in France to parents from the Antilles, combining *nègre* with *hexagonale*,
which refers to the hexagonal shape of France.

NAOMI HAD HARDLY BEEN CONVINCED BY PASSIONISE'S LOGIC. By now, she was honestly having a hard time following their conversation. From anecdotes to grand theories, from jokes to empirically based axioms, each was sharing her own experience, barely listening to the others, grasping only scraps of what they were saying, picking up on an insignificant detail, a word, a syllable even—the way Éleuthéra had—in order to make a pun or bring everything back to herself, each refocusing the conversation onto her own little self, not really caring what the others meant, what they were bemoaning or shouting or crying or teasing about. To Naomi, the entire thing sounded rather disjointed. The TV—firmly set to Channel One with a notice that read "Do not change the channel" and turned on to help patients be more patient in the waiting room—was airing a documentary. Naomi opted to lose herself in her thoughts and, rather conspicuously, dropped out of the conversation. The others immediately carried on.

"Using robots to graft roses! What's next, robots sending roses to women as well?" Félixe's frightening question was frustratingly left unanswered. With a smile on her face, Espélisane continued.

"In any case, I know some men who would appreciate having robots—or rather clones—to present roses to their women on Valentine's Day and Mother's Day. Since on those days, some have their hands full. Each year, one of them begins seeing stars after bringing roses to his galaxy of girlfriends, having been made to drink three dozen glasses of champagne of varying quality, and worse, having blown up his liver from being forced, when he was already full, to scarf down three dozen slices of coconut cake—a mont-blanc, they all know it's his favorite—while acting like a glutton and pretending to be on cloud nine. For Mussieu Macho, the mandatory tasting of the seventh homemade mont-blanc is more agonizing than climbing Mont Blanc—the grated coconut snowflakes stick to his palate and teeth, and he swears never again; next year in early February and again in late May, he'll escape to Cuba, on the pretext of going hunting, even if it's not the season. But for now, he's stuck. Blocked. A mighty fisherman before the Lord— and proud to be—he's now caught in the net, having fallen into the trap of a network of lady friends that he himself created. He's now condemned to the torment he brought upon himself. This is the *coqueur*'s calvary. They crucify him, these pairs of eyes that spy on him, lie in wait for him, don't let him go (if only the poor souls knew!). They see to it that everything goes smoothly, and worse, pour their man some rum; well, that's the last straw! If only they knew how bad their beau is feeling: he's got heartburn and everything hurts—tummy, head, everywhere—despite the sweet kisses forming a crown of thorns on his sweat-soaked forehead, or *on account of that crown of kisses*. The guy cries tears of sweat. His women think he's feverish, lavish attention on him. It goes from bad to worse. The man suffers. The macho suffers agonies. The scoundrel goes from Charybdis to Scylla. The more they bustle about, the more he suffers. The more they hover, coddle him, knock themselves out cooking and offering him a pick-me-up, the more they make his head spin; he's going to vomit. The lascar's belly is about to burst, all the booze is going to his head. For women in Martinique, Mother's Day and Valentine's Day are days of vengeance: unconscious, innocent, and quite legitimate."

Hanging on to Espélisane's words from her plump yet prophetic lips, Laetitia stares in amazement.

"Those guys would love to be able to clone themselves or have the gift of being everywhere at once on these holidays, these auspicious days that are inauspicious for them," the *métisse* continues, on a roll. "Mother's Day in Martinique is the macho's marathon, the major's martyrology, what do you think? You've got to see them! You're from France, Laetitia, so you don't know, but you've got to see it! The guy has to visit—in order of priority—his mother, grandmother, godmother, the woman who carried him to the baptismal font, and then his series of 'baby mamas'—all the women who, in turn, or at the same time, have 'given him a *ti manmaille*'—*doudous* of all colors, sizes, ages, or else replicas of the same model (a registered design, for some, that only comes in chubby; light-skinned *chabine*; slender, darker *capresse*; or callipygian *bonda maté*), menopausal *grandes dames*, *métropolitaines* from mainland France, or mature women of black-white ancestry, young things or nymphets: he's up by the time the rooster crows. It's even worse on Valentine's Day, since he has to fake being *in love!* Mussieu Macho plays the part of the *co-coo-er*, this coqueur, billing and cooing. This is the coqueur's calvary. Fourteen stations of the cross? If only. It's more like thirty, at the very least, for the average Valentine, *zanzoling* and zigzagging, in danger of ending up in a ditch.

"That's what Mother's Day and Valentine's Day mean for machos in Martinique. By the end of both days, they go home bankrupt and broken. If you ever run into one of them at the end of one of these disastrous days, just keep moving. There's nothing left to get out of him. He's cleaned out the flower shops, emptied his pouch, in every sense of the word—depleted both the ATMs and all his strength. He's out of service. The major-in-chief is out of service, like the ATMs. His seed pods are empty, his belly full, the trunk of his *Merde*cedes-Benz cleared out, strewn with the wilted petals from all the bunches of flowers, desecrated because they were given so hastily, on the fly, to one here, one there, then another one and still another, poor bouquets, battered throughout the whole blessed day along the roads of Martinique. Nothing of his stays upright anymore—especially not the most important part of his anatomy. Paunch overloaded like a surette tree with berries used for pig feed, he can't even get raunchy; he's got nothing to unload."

Her gaze fixed on Espélisane, Laetitia laps up everything she says. "Oh really?"

"So much so that Mussieu Big Appetite was no longer hungry, not even one bit, after his umpteenth Mother's Day meal. You should have seen him when he arrived at my neighbor's: the lady flipped out! I swear, you could hear her all the way from Grand-Rivière to Morne Larcher."

Now Roxélane joins the fun.

"*Tchip!* A novice! A coqueur-in-training. The smartest, most duplicitous guys make themselves vomit between rendezvous. It's quite an art."

"Yuck!"

"The swine do worry themselves sick, after all," Espélisane declares, unrepentant.

"But the cocks who've earned their stripes make a point to go peck at all of their lady friends and no scandal ever breaks out."

Espélisane relishes explaining it all to Laetitia the *Nègzagonale* and spares no detail:

"My dear, I'm not making this up. In this country, Mother's Day and Valentine's Day are a real ordeal for the average Antillean man, the atavistic coqueur, the fucker with a finger in every pie, who behaves in such an open, obvious, systemic way that it's almost no longer cheating.

"It's the coqueur's calvary and the macho's motorized marathon. Mother's Day is the macho's marathon, given that the mothers of his children are spread all over the island. He's made mothers of so many women for miles around, distributing miles of his rod—enough to turn any of their bellies round. He's traveled so extensively, sleeping around and cutting through hills, ravines and savannas, suburbs and residential neighborhoods, affordable housing complexes, luxury villas and humble shacks, without discrimination or prejudice of skin color, and on this day he's forced to visit each one of these *manmans,* who every time has prepared a good *bwè-manjé* for her man, cooked in her small matriarchal unit. She's lovingly simmered the holiday meal and knocked herself out with the cooking; she believes—or wants to believe—that she's the only one. And since he's there, he has to eat. In the end, his breadbasket is full. With champagne flowing to celebrate these multiple agapes—in fact, *agapê* in Greek means 'love,' 'affection,' 'meal shared in perfect communion'—because Guadeloupe and Martinique are the world champions in champagne consumption, at the end of the day, the guy keels over, wasted. And at Christmas, same *bagay*! It's the major's martyrology, among a string of boudins in all hues and a bevy of babies in all colors as well."

Bewildered, idealistic, and disconcerted, Laetitia, aka Miss Gaiety, recaps, out of chronological order: "So on Valentine's Day, Christmas, and Mother's Day, it's the macho's marathon, the major's martyrology, and the coqueur's calvary," as she sees her dreams of an exclusive love and her sweet Nègzagonale illusions unravelling.

"What a competitive display of hypocrisy on both sides," reckons Vésuviana, sleeping with one eye open. "Because most of them close their eyes and open their thighs without any apparent qualms."

"That can't be, you're exaggerating," groans Miss Gaiety, flustered.

"Well, I'm not exaggerating when I say Valentine's Day is the worst. Because on top of everything else, on Valentine's Day, our man must look like he's in love. And prove it. His rod better be in shape. In the worst case, since the dates for Mardi Gras change each year, he's hardly finished with Carnival, where his *cal* has seen a lot of action—he's barely emptied out his seed pods here—when February 14 comes and he has to start afresh elsewhere, again and again. He's got to bang, bang, bang, and bang again until his prick unscrews. Some achieve a priapic aplomb, without the help of any medical adjuvants or small blue pills, and most reach the end of their marathon without any doping. But watch out for Miss Persistent who'll go as far as asking him to open the trunk of his car on some pretext or another: said trunk is packed with bouquets and champagne bottles—as many in there as he has women out there. See, *i pwan fè! Yo pwan fè!* They're both in trouble! The audacious ladylove who is too inquisitive risks a beating. Because these cheaters can't stand being trapped or cheated on. That's the number one rule. No jealous fits unless you want to put your life on the line. The more the guy cheats, the less he tolerates being cheated on or being suspected of infidelity, and the more jealous and possessive he himself gets. It's almost mathematical. The level of jealousy is generally proportional to the level of infidelity. I speak from personal experience, seen it with my own eyes. A *batte-manman*. A *ouélélé*. Enough to blow a pharaonic gasket during this pantagruelian escapade. That's how it's been since the Marquis d'Antin. The guy has such a bad conscience that the slightest question feels like the Spanish Inquisition—tormented, he takes it out on the imprudent impudent who's interrogating him, who dares to ask where's he's been, where he's going, and with whom."

"Yes, I've seen it, too, with my own eyes, I tell you. It was late in the day one Mother's Day. A father who'd probably gone through the traditional obstacle course had, for better or worse, gulped down several festive meals during the day and filled up on drinks. He still insisted on attending Sunday night vespers at Bellevue Church. He showed up a good half hour late, staggering and nodding. And would you believe that, right in the middle of the service, the guy relieved the fullness of his stomach and puked profusely on the parishioner seated in front of him..."

"I can't believe it," sobs Miss Gaiety, more disgusted by the male chauvinist triad than by its emetic effects.

"But today there are certain kinds of women who are changing things. They are polygamous—or rather, polyandrous—because it's not about marriage here, and they have a pleiad of guys—*anêr, andros,* meaning 'man' in Greek—so they compartmentalize and manage to arrange things so they can host each 'André' in turn, without any of them suspecting they're far from being the one and only. Some of them are really quite talented and highly organized, boss ladies who have updated the status of simple mistress. They are the worthy successors of the former matadors from Saint-Pierre and of the *Dame aux Camélias*, written by Alexandre Dumas fils, himself a descendant of an Antillean woman who was born in what is now called Haiti. Coincidence? Connection? There are no coincidences, only connections—devilishly Baudelairean connections. We can never say it enough. Didn't Baudelaire have a splenic relationship with Jeanne Duval, a métisse actress originally from Haiti, a woman of black-white ancestry who was his muse and had a profuse libido?"

"Some women are also so sophisticated as to give each of their partners the same nickname—how practical! This way, there's no chance of being caught, no risk of getting it wrong when they cry out, in the throes of passion, the same name— one for all, all for one—and that's all there is to it. 'André, André, oh André!' while swooning. Of course, it's an André, *anêr*, *andros*, no one the wiser, she's impudent, impenitent, unpunished."

"These guys don't hesitate to use this kind of tactic. Why can't women do the same?"

"I know one, one of these guys perpetually in love, whose wife's name was Ghislaine. One fine day he became infatuated with another Ghislaine. She was a once-in-a-lifetime opportunity, as well as his passion of the moment! Thus, he could pride himself on purring 'Ghislaine, oh Ghislaine' in his lawful wife's ear at the height of lovemaking, while dreaming with impunity of her namesake."

"It's tempting to apply to the letter the pseudo-Asian instructions that the friendly Chinese restaurant owner from Terres-Sainville dispenses to women: For starters, it's important, even paramount, to find a man who helps you with housework and tough chores, and who has a good job. Second, it's important, or at least desirable, to find a witty man with a good sense of humor, who makes you laugh. Third, it's important, and even indispensable, to find a man you can rely on and trust, and who never lies to you. Fourth, it's important, and even crucial, to find a man who can show empathy and understanding—but not too much—not to the point of reading you like an open book. Fifth, it's important, indeed imperative, to find a man who's good in bed, who likes making love to you. Sixth, it's important, and even vital, that these men don't know one another, and fundamental that they never meet."

"To be precise, it's indisputable," adds Roxélane, à la Thompson and Thomson, Hergé's comic book detectives.

"Otherwise, watch out for a fistfight!"

"Yes and with the blessing of the Judiciary, totally unjust from time immemorial, from the darkest days when obscurantism was the rule of the day, codified and institutionalized, well before the misogynistic Napoleonic Code, in tenebrous times such as under the Visigoths' Roman law, which blithely stipulated that 'a husband is allowed to conduct an inquiry into his wife's adultery by torturing each spouse's slaves—that is, his own and his wife's slaves—but only if it were proven that they were, at that moment, at the place or in the house where the adultery was suspected to have taken place.' These aren't old wives' tales, or the delusions of raging anti-slavery feminists: This was written and clearly spelled out in black and white in the *Theodosiani libricum constitutionibus Sirmondianis* dating back to the sixth century. The Visigoths weren't playing around back then when it came to women or slaves! It goes on to say: 'Any free woman who secretly has sex with her own slave should be sentenced to death. As for the slave who was convicted of adultery with his mistress, let him be set on fire. Anyone wishing to make an accusation regarding this type of criminal behavior has the power to do so. Even slaves or servants must be heard in this regard, insofar as they will be granted freedom if they provide evidence and will be punished if they've lied. The inheritance of the woman who's defiled herself with such a crime must be distributed among her sons, if they were conceived by her husband, or among his blood relatives, in the order prescribed by the law [...]. If a slave dies while his master administers punishment, the master will not be found guilty of homicide unless there is proof of the master's intention to kill. A beating should not be considered a crime.' Not a word on the husband's adultery."

"Not much changed between then and the period of slavery in the Antilles. In 1804, Napoleon Bonaparte, as Emperor, having reinstated slavery two years earlier as First Consul and perpetrated this ultimate crime against humanity, then also perpetuated the 'infinite bondage' of women by enacting the Civil Code, aka 'Napoleonic Code,' which institutionalized the confinement of women to the domestic sphere. Until 1970, they were considered minors and subjected to the authority of a father or husband. The Civil Code thereby sanctioned the total legal incapacity of the married woman, who was considered forever a minor (and only a major with regard to her faults). Women were denied access to high schools and universities, forbidden to sign contracts or manage their assets, denied their political rights, forbidden to work without spousal authorization or collect their own salary, subjected to spousal control over correspondence and relationships, and forbidden to travel abroad without permission."

"The Napoleonic Code was also extremely repressive regarding women's adultery. Unwed mothers and illegitimate children had no rights, and a married woman had to automatically adopt her husband's nationality."

"And this Code became even stricter in 1810 when it came to women: The adulterous woman could be punished by imprisonment, while the adulterous man only risked a simple fine. Conjugal duties were an obligation, rape between spouses didn't exist, and to add insult to injury, the penal code allowed for stiff sentences against abortions."

Passionise, the Golden Chabine, couldn't care less about what the others thought: "In his defense, a notorious—but nonetheless adorable—coqueur once said, 'So much love spread around, so much love that would have gone to waste.'"

"Some have no shame and some of the bold ones serve up the excuse that 'there are more women than men in Martinique,' delighted that Martinique has the lowest male-to-female ratio in the world. While the worldwide average is 101.8 men per 100 women, this French island reports 84.5 men per 100 women. This large proportion of women remains unexplained but is used as a convenient justification by coqueurs and their ilk. There are even some who hide behind the aftermath of the Code Noir. Slavery is a convenient scapegoat! After all this time! Don't tell me it's because slaves weren't entitled to form real families, or because owners could sell children and parents separately, or because owners were the legal owners of slave bodies, and because settlers enjoyed the *droit du seigneur* on their slaves, that today these men who sow children all over the place are not a disgrace and can release themselves of all paternal responsibilities. Fortunately, they're an endangered species! We're lucky that things are changing; signs of upright women are popping up. This restores the balance and may well succeed in reestablishing harmony. That's my wish for us!"

"Yeah, right! There are some women who encourage this behavior."

"We can't generalize," Naomi murmurs, marooning in all directions, muttering and freeing herself of preconceived ideas.

Espélisane doesn't fail to pick up on Naomi's laconic, indulgent remark. "Yes, we should be careful not to generalize. Fortunately, they're not all raging coqueurs. Admittedly, these guys are a dime a dozen, and their practices are flourishing—not only among straight men—but there are still quite a few who are neither coqueurs, machos, womanizers, skirt chasers, players, cheaters, Don Juans, nor Casanovas. All the same, let's be realistic: All these words are dated but the practice is not. Far from it. Most of these words are obsolete but the realities they represent are forever *à la mode*, hip, very trendy, 'in,' cool, fresh, *au courant*—a long, long time after the actual words and the terms have ended up on the scrap heap and are no longer in vogue. Infidelity is everywhere, inside and outside of marriage, in cohabitation and domestic partnerships. We no longer talk about unscrupulous seducers, ladies' men, and even less of guys in search of hanky panky. The words are gone, but the acts remain, the praxis persists, *krakrakra*," she cackles.

"'Sigh no more, ladies, sigh no more. Men were deceivers ever, one foot in sea, and one on shore, to one thing constant never. Then sigh not so, but let them go, and be you blithe and bonny, converting all your sounds of woe... Sing no more ditties, sing no more of dumps so dull and heavy. The fraud of men was ever so since summer first was leafy. Then sigh not so...' I didn't make this up, it's Shakespeare...*Much Ado About Nothing*. Ah, high school memories! At the time, I used to know the English text by heart," says Roxélane, daydreaming.

"What I remember is 'let them go, and be you blithe and bonny.'"

"'Swiss cheese skin, let the men pass through!' as the old Creole song goes..."

"Nonetheless, Valentine's Day 'under the tropical sun' isn't only the coqueur's calvary and the macho's marathon. In the Antilles, this date takes on entirely different meanings. In Guadeloupe, the Valentine's Day Massacre took place on February 14, 1952. Let's remember Constance Dulac, Capitolin Justinien, François Serdot, and Édouard Dernon, who would surely have preferred being hit by Cupid's arrows than by the deadly bullets of the French riot squad."

Propitiatory anamnesis, refusal to obey the injunction to forget, not masking the past to keep moving forward. That February 14, in the town of Le Moule, the workers of the Gardel factory organized a strike to demand higher wages. Barricades were erected by strikers on the picket line. The French law enforcement agencies deployed on-site were ordered to open fire on the crowd. The toll: four dead and fourteen wounded.

Back then, they shot. There was no Prefect Grimaud—degreed in literature and a keen reader of Gide and Proust, who later became the "cop boss"—to disregard De Gaulle's awful ukase from May 1968, declaring you had to be able to order firing on demonstrators, namely on French students.

Éleuthéra's ears are ringing from the barking of Ogoun Ferraille's psychic dog. The metallic and omniscient, hyper-mnesic and cathartic barking helps stir up the consciousness and the reappropriation of a History and a Memory quite different from what she was taught in school. Through the Iron Dog's intercession, she suddenly has a vision of the Gardel factory blood bath, both in black and white and in technicolor, as if she'd actually experienced it, even though she hadn't been born yet.

The movement had begun in November 1951 in the north of Grande-Terre. The strikers were demanding better pay and less strenuous work in the fields of the whites, the *békés*. They were asking for salaries on par with the French workers, referring to the Law of March 16, 1946, that granted the colonies in the Antilles the status of French administrative departments. Then the demands expanded to include raising the price per ton of sugarcane.

In early 1952, civil servants joined the strikers, demanding higher salaries. A call for a general strike was issued all over Guadeloupe. Most of the sugarcane production sites were involved: Petit-Bourg, Capesterre, Comté, Beauport, Bonne Mère...

On February 11, the riot squad took up position in the town of Le Moule, the only port on the Atlantic coast, and where several sugar factories and rum distilleries were located at the time. On February 14, 1952, the strikers erected a barricade at the entrance of Boulevard Rougé to prevent sugarcane carts from entering the Gardel factory.

The riot squad opened fire on the unarmed crowd. Four Guadeloupeans were killed and fourteen seriously wounded. Some of the victims, innocent bystanders or nosey passersby, had no ties with either the social movement or the demonstrators.

"Every February 14, commemorative events are organized by Guadeloupe's political groups and unions. A memorial stone was erected in front of the cemetery in Le Moule, and an odonym, Rue du 14-Février-1952, serves as a local reminder of these tragic events."

"A nodo-what?"

"An odonym. You know, a street name. Rue du 14-Février-1952."

"Sorry for being a spoilsport, but it's important for us here in the Antilles to remember that February 14 represents much more than a lovers' celebration; it's a somber date. Because that's not all! Quick reminder: a little over 'twenty years after'—to paraphrase our cousin Alexandre Dumas, a multiracial man from Saint-Domingue (the future Haiti)— there was another Valentine's Day Massacre, this one taking place in Martinique on February 14, 1974, amid a context of heightened social unrest. Rénor Ilmany, a fifty-five-year-old employee at a banana plantation, demanded higher wages, a total ban on toxic products, and improved working conditions. He was killed by gendarmes on the grounds of the Habitation Chalvet plantation in Basse-Pointe. Two days later, on February 16, nineteen-year-old Georges Marie-Louise was found dead on a beach not far from where the first killing took place. His body showed signs of torture. These are two key dates in the history of the fight for social justice and the evolution of the trade union movement in Martinique."

At this juncture, in an effort to lift Miss Gaiety's obviously low spirits, Éleuthéra makes an effort to revisit the coqueur's calvary and the macho's marathon.

The charmer in every sense of the word—that is, the lover of many, but also the cunning guy you can't trust—had more than a few tricks up his sleeve (and more than one dress shirt in his car trunk). The spare shirt, identical in every way to the one he had on when he left in the morning, is the seasoned macho's lifesaver. He buys these shirts in bulk; some distinguished coqueurs even hide a few in their offices.

No matter his social status, the professional coqueur always has half a dozen shirts in his trunk. If only she knew—the one who devotedly ironed them—what these immaculate shirts were used for... The sins they concealed... Could she in fact know full well? It's certainly not impossible; she may even, perhaps, on some level, be secretly proud of it—that her rascal has several women. "This is proof of his success," she may sob on occasion, a resigned *potomitan* woman, upright in her resignation.

The myth of the potomitan woman, this pillar of strength, conceals the tremendous power of the unspoken and of the disguised phallocracy masquerading as a so-called matriarchy that is nothing but matrifocality, conveniently enough for these men, who are therefore released of all responsibilities.

"Where there's love, there's never darkness," whispers the Psychic Dog, verbose with African proverbs, whether authentic or made up on the spot.

But Éleuthéra doesn't give in to the voice. To hear her talk, the high-spirited one is getting close to practicing a *sui-generis* form of realpolitik.

And then, after affirming in a booming voice, *"Kouté pou tann, tann pou konprann* (listen so you hear, hear so you understand)," Félixe, aka Two Drum Beats, delights in telling the story of the betrayed woman who says to her extremely wealthy husband, "Ours is prettier," as she assesses the neighbor's mistress. She herself refuses to get divorced, determined to hold on to her lavish lifestyle.

"No need to repeat old misogynistic jokes *à la* Sacha Guitry," Espélisane protests, half-heartedly. "Those days are over!"

"That's what you think!" Éleuthéra feels compelled to lament. "At the turn of the twenty-first century, we're at the edge of the jungle. The rich get richer, and the poor get poorer, and gold-digging women are far from being an endangered species. Coats made of real panther fur will disappear much sooner, as they're a much less protected species."

"In fact, the most phallocratic and misogynistic sentence there ever was is disguised as a pseudo tribute to Women: 'Behind every great man there's a great woman.' And why not a great man behind every great woman? Try switching the terms and you'll measure the magnitude of machismo. A jokester even wrote: 'Behind every great man hides a woman with nothing to wear,'" Roxélane chuckles.

"At the turn of the twenty-first century, as you say, Espélisane, let's 'harvest the present day'—to paraphrase Horace with pertinence and impertinence—but let's also worry about the future, because here and elsewhere, yesterday and today and tomorrow, the fight for women's rights begun by Olympe de Gouges, among others, is always ongoing. 'Women have the right to mount the scaffold; they must also have the right to mount the speaker's rostrum.' Since Olympe de Gouges, battles have been won, words have flowed freely, brave denouncements of spousal abuse and workplace harassment, which is still pervasive, not to mention unequal pay for equal work or the fight for the right to become a mother, without that hindering your career advancement, especially for female executives."

"Even in the American film industry, tarnished by the Weinstein scandal, you still find the same type of predator who's been on the prowl for ages. People—even world celebrities—thought he was 'too big to fail,' to borrow the expression coined by the American media during the 2008 economic crisis: the toxic financial arrangements of global banks. He was too big in the literal and metaphorical sense of the word, and too powerful financially to fail! The opposite was proven by women who banded together in large numbers to bring him down, by taking to court this world-famous producer, the most influential in Hollywood. Even so, the American film industry didn't die. In fact, it emerged even stronger for it—a fitting reversal for an industry that focuses on glamour and creates icons. Thanks initially to the #MeToo movement on social media, and later in traditional media, those who had long protected this prestigious producer—blinded by his omnipotence and convinced that his word was truth and that all the women were lying—finally opened their eyes."

Whatever the outcome of this corpulent vulture's trial, nothing would ever be the same.

"But as Simone de Beauvoir noted in her time, many things can also regress due to the obscurantist dogma of malicious male spirits and even—much to my dismay—to spineless, reactionary, or even misogynistic female mentalities, not to mention religion and religious fanaticism, which are pervasive in this twenty-first century."

"Here you feel like shouting, 'O my body, always make me philosophize in a way that brings to mind Frantz Fanon!'"

"So then, CARPE DIEM! Let's hope that 2019 brings serenity and, without being too ingenuous, some optimism, assuming we remain vigilant and vindictive, like Jacqueline Sauvage, who succeeded in getting people to recognize she had nothing to be ashamed of, that she wasn't the tormenter, and that she had to save her children from lifelong trauma."

"Because it's not only the body of women that's being assaulted—it's the very body of society. All of humankind must safeguard itself by protecting those who represent a good half of it."

"Human beings have been writing since ancient times, inscribing on stone, papyrus, parchment, and then on paper. Reading works wonders (provided men actually do read, because obscurantism springs from illiteracy)."

Eventually, at Laetitia's insistence, Espélisane shares the epilogue to the marathon of the *mapipi* macho who slithered his way into taking the prize on Valentine's Day:

After multiple feasts, Mussieu Macho rushed to take refuge in his lawful wife's skirts and dozed off. However, while he was asleep, this lawful wife deprived the motorized centaur—powered by his engine's mighty horses—not only of his means of locomotion but also of his means of fornication. Suspecting the multi-purpose use of Mussieu Macho's vehicle, she stole the key while he was napping. Up the creek without a paddle, our professional coqueur was stalled for quite some time.

But the worst came later, when this devilish guy, under the influence of a notorious mid-life crisis that some say comes from Satan himself, attempted to have sex with a minor—an act he described as "romantic"—driving to the home of his daughter's high-school friend with the intention of deflowering her. He thought it very chivalrous, with a hint of romance.

Mussieu Macho only lifts his buttocks from the driver's seat to visit this or that woman's place to get laid. Without his car, he's nothing. His power is measured in horsepower and summed up in a taxable horsepower rating. A modern monster, part man, part beast, with the strength of a thousand horses in his head and in his briefs, the motorized centaur —aka Major Coqueur—found himself in a pickle when a cloudburst came and he was unable to get into his car. In his haste to leave the house of the deflowered minor to escape the strict *pater familias* who'd come home earlier than expected, he'd barely had time to leave through the verandah, wearing nothing but boxer shorts, practically stark naked under the downpour, leaving his pants behind in his precipitation. His keys were in the pocket. He used all the curse words he knew, both in Creole and in French, two languages that his outrageously expensive vehicle—not a millennial car, to say the least—had no command of; it remained stubbornly locked, turning a deaf ear to all injunctions to unlock. The buffoon swore and vowed to buy himself a high-tech marvel equipped with voice-activated doors or digital unlocking—anything, as long as it unlocked, godammit!

Childishly, this guy dreamed of a car that would instantly react to his slightest whistle, just like Zorro's horse, and would arrive pronto, doors unlocked. He'd buy himself one for Christmas. Or, resolutely immature and devoid of any guilt, he would get the most gullible of his women to buy it for him— someone who'd be willing to take out a large loan so as not to lose her little angel.

Pointe-des-Nègres—a district of Fort-de-France, the landing place for slaves deported from Africa during the slave trade, bordering on the town of Schœlcher—named after a leading figure in the abolition of slavery—o armada of symbols! But there are no coincidences, only connections—Baudelairean connections.

February 2020, in memoriam, celebrating the 226th anniversary of the abolition of slavery on February 4, 1794, during the French Revolution by the National Convention, thereby duly recording the victorious uprising of the men and women enslaved in the French part of the island of Saint-Domingue (now the Republic of Haiti, "where negritude rose for the first time and stated that it believed in its humanity," dixit Césaire).

GERTY DAMBURY

Defiant Islands

TRANSLATED BY JUDITH MILLER AND GERTY DAMBURY

Je suis éprise d'un pays-ombre.

I.

I am in exile from an unborn country.
I chose to stride across a fiction.
The island I hope for is a hidden dream.
Secretly, I name it. Unknown, its location and value.
No caravel sets sail toward it; not one shameful ship.
Palpable chimera, it reveals itself then capsizes.
A traveler's hallucination.
I am in love with an invisible land.
A simulacre of land smelling of legend.
A wasteland, yearning for yesterday, bursting with yesteryear,
    aware of pains to come.
I build it up, gigantic in me, but a comma on the ocean—though
    with the wings of a sea hawk and the lightness of an osprey.

I am from there that won't be seen.
On my fantasy acres, I grow antique tobacco,
And my lair quivers with pleasure.

Stationed on a maritime ruse, I watch the movement of
    the ships.
The winds are my allies or perhaps victims of my charm:
    they do not speak my presence.
The dogs muzzle my traces.
I am from there that can no longer be heard.

I do not voice my pain and I veil my dead. Other humans pass
    in the distance.
Their thirst, their need to re-provision leave me indifferent.
Staying out of history? This, my blood will praise one day.
May he who might shred my children on the point of his sword
    never discover me.
I come from a dream he cannot ever share.

I instructed my witches:
Sculpt the haze and the sea spray,
Never leave a trace of your art,
Chisel your figurines by night so that by daybreak they vanish.
Cover the prints of your feet.
I instructed my sirens:
Sing your songs only within your selves, spiraling intimacy.
Keep your voices' beauty from waylaying sailors.
Become those whom the blood suspects, whose absence

makes the winds shiver and shudder—but barely.
Barely a trouble at all.

Alas, my tongue was burning to share the beauty,
Insisting its passion be envied.
How does one praise the charms of anonymous grace?
Make desirable a parable island?
An insolent fantasmatic soil?
Caves without etchings, imaginary people?

I set tables on the seas as a sign of welcome.
I moved the threshold of my cabin to the shore.
Fresh water erupted from my welcoming hands.
Here, drink, this is my memory.
And this, my amnesty.

Crazy recidivist...
Everything escaped from me.
Prophets wanted to dictate my dreams.
Wisdom, with a smile, urged me to let them go
"What's the value of a dream someone else sketches in your night?"

II.

So sorry, it just slipped out!
I couldn't keep it safe in locked mouth and clenched teeth.
The flow erupted from my lips.
Pinched lips, tongue tucked toward the throat, toward
    the glottis,
Tongue rolled around itself, as though swallowed.
"... *they swallowed their tongues to escape from hell...*"
Mouth closely guarded
Words missing, hidden
All expression repressed.

But sorry, it slipped out!
I couldn't control my salivary glands,
Three pairs of overproducing glands,
Parotid and sublingual.
Mandibles contracted.
"...*they bequeathed aching jaws to their newborns*
by piercing the fontanel with a needle..."
An ache invisible from above
And below the jaws.
Just a very small pain.
Turn the tongue seven times in the mouth

And the cavity will fill with liquid.

Oh, sorry, it just slipped out!
In the beginning a stream of water, ions, urea
Basically, a rivulet of digestive juices
Patiently swelled the silence in my throat.
I stopped lowering my lingual bone
No more swallowing.
Buccal cavity inundated.
I drown myself softly in my saliva
That rises, saturating the buccal cavity,
Immersing my teeth, my soft palate, my palatine tonsils
Expanding, expanding.

And then, it's no longer a stream.
It's a river, a waterway
My mouth can no longer contain.
Thousands of very tiny balls of spit
Rolled under my tongue,
When,

General Dugommier
Your words are in my head:
"Here is what I think about this country:

We must destroy all Negroes in the mountains, men and women..."
Your words are in my head
And in my mouth a very tiny ball of spit.
"...only spare the children younger than twelve..."
When I walk up the street of my childhood that carries your name,
Your words are in my head.
"...destroy half of those on the plain..."
I don't know yet that this tiny ball of spit that hears you
"...and leave not one single man in the colony who has worn a uniform..."
This tiny little ball of spit that gets bigger with your words
"...without that, the colony will never be pacified..."

I don't know yet that this tiny little ball of spit that hears you
The tiny little ball of spit that gets bigger
Will birth...

Sorry, it just slipped out!
A moving mass vacates the chasm in me.
That pit of bodies buried
Century after century.
An ocean of my saliva
Spills into the streets and the squares
Washes over the silence.
The tiny little ball of spit of my childhood

Now grown big
Is from now on a flood impossible to contain.
It pours out in grandiose cascades
Thundering falls,
Swirling rapids,
Waves that howl, walls of water!
I open my mouth and without a word
I unleash torrents.

Contributors

Marie-Célie Agnant was born in 1953 in Port-au-Prince, Haiti, and has lived in Canada since 1970. Her writings include four novels, two short story collections, and three volumes of poetry. She has also worked as a storyteller, an interpreter, a teacher, and an environmental activist. In her literary works, she offers lyrical explorations of the unsaid, legacies of violence and loss in families and societies consumed by memories they share in silence. She received the Prix Alain-Grandbois of the Académie des Lettres du Québec in 2017 for her most recent collection of poetry, *Femmes de terres brûlées* (2016). In 2023, she was appointed Canada's tenth Parliamentary Poet Laureate.

Adlyne Bonhomme is a native of Les Palmes in Petit-Goâve, Haiti. In 2017, she edited a collection of poetry in memory of the victims of Hurricane Matthew entitled *Écrire pour ne pas oublier*. In 2019, she published *L'Éternité des cathédrales*, a collection of fragmentary and erotic poems, with Éditions de la Rosée. She has participated in various literary festivals in Haiti, such as the Marathon du Livre, and she actively contributes to online literary reviews, including *Plimay*.

Nancy Naomi Carlson is a poet and translator whose translation of Khal Torabully's *Cargo Hold of Stars: Coolitude* (Seagull Books, 2021) won the Oxford-Weidenfeld Translation Prize. Decorated with the French Academic Palms and twice awarded NEA literature translation grants, she's the author of *An Infusion of Violets* (Seagull Books, 2019), named "New & Noteworthy" by *The New York Times*. She's the translation editor for *On the Seawall*.

Gerty Dambury is a noted playwright, novelist, poet, theater director, and performer, as well as a cultural activist. She has lived and worked between Guadeloupe—her home and also an overseas department of France—and France. She has recently moved to Britany, where she is working on establishing an arts complex that will help promote works by Black artists, mostly Caribbean.

Nathan H. Dize is a reader, researcher, and translator of Haitian and Afro-Diasporic literatures in French. He is the translator of three novels: *The Immortals* by Makenzy Orcel (SUNY Press, 2020), *I Am Alive* by Kettly Mars (UVA Press, 2022), and *Antoine of Gommiers* by Lyonel Trouillot (Schaffner Press, 2023). He has also translated poetry by Charles Moravia, James Noël, and Évelyne Trouillot. He teaches French at Washington University in Saint Louis.

Suzanne Dracius, prizewinning author and playwright from Martinique, was hailed by the French Cultural Minister as "one of the great figures of Antillean letters." Dracius' work explores Martinique's complex cultural history, as well as the identity of those born in the former French colonies in the Caribbean but raised in mainland France, not feeling at home in either place due to the color of their skin. Her sophisticated language is peppered with Creole, word play, Latin, slang, and neologisms.

Eric Fishman is an educator, writer, and translator. His most recent translation is *Outside: Poetry and Prose* by André du Bouchet (Bitter Oleander Press). He is currently translating a selected volume of poetry by Monchoachi. Eric is also a founding editor of *Young Radish*, a magazine of poetry and art by kids and teens.

Dawn Fulton teaches French and comparative literature at Smith College. Her translation of Marie-Célie Agnant's novella *Silence Like Blood* was published in the *Massachusetts Review*'s Working Titles series in 2020. She has received a PEN/Heim Translation Fund Grant for the translation of Michèle Lacrosil's 1961 novel *Cajou*.

Danielle Legros Georges is the author of *The Dear Remote Nearness of You* (2016) and translator of *Island Heart* (2021), a collection of poems of Haitian-French writer Ida Faubert, among other titles. Her poems have been widely published, anthologized, and included in international artistic commissions and collaborations. In 2014, Legros Georges was named Boston's poet laureate. She is a professor of creative writing at Lesley University.

Kaiama L. Glover is a writer, translator, and Ann Whitney Olin Professor of French and Africana Studies at Barnard College, as well as founding coeditor of the journal *archipelagos*. She is the translator of *Ready to Burst* by Frankétienne (Archipelago, 2014), *Dance on the Volcano* by Marie Vieux-Chauvet (Archipelago, 2017), *Hadriana in All My Dreams* by René Depestre (Akashic Books, 2017), and *Sweet Undoings* by Yanick Lahens (Deep Vellum, 2023) among other titles.

Mireille Jean-Gilles, born in French Guiana in 1962, is an agroeconomist. Wife of the poet Monchoachi, she currently lives in Martinique and works on the financial problems of the French overseas collectivities. She holds tight to words and numbers with equal passion, always in search of a poem. Her most recent collection tracks the character of the woman in the "voracious street."

Born in France to Caribbean parents, **Fabienne Kanor** is a writer and filmmaker whose novels include *D'eaux douces*, *Humus*, *Je ne suis pas un homme qui pleure*, and *Louisiane*. Her works interrogate race and gender in France and the French Antilles, and West African migrations to France. Awarded the Chevalier des Arts & des Lettres and the 2020 Casa de Las Americas Prize, Kanor is a professor of French and Francophone Studies at Penn State.

Born and raised in France, **Catherine Maigret Kellogg** discovered a passion for literary translation when working with Nancy Naomi Carlson on a co-translation of Suzanne Dracius' novel *L'Autre qui danse*. Leaving aside her marketing career, she obtained a master's degree in translation from Université Sorbonne-Nouvelle in Paris and now works for a translation company. Excerpts from *The Dancing Other* have been published in *The New England Review* and *The Massachusetts Review*.

Kettly Mars is an award-winning Francophone writer from Port-au-Prince, Haiti, who has been producing short stories, poems, and novels since the mid-1990s. Her work has been translated into Danish, Dutch, English, German, Italian, and Japanese. Her most recent novel, *The Patriarch's Angel*, is a thriller about a cursed Haitian family and explores the conflict between vodou culture and Christian culture in modern-day Haiti.

Judith G. Miller is professor emerita of French and Francophone theater at New York University. In addition to publishing widely on contemporary theater production, notably on Francophone African theater and the Théâtre du Soleil, she has translated some thirty plays from the French and a novel by Gerty Dambury, *The Restless* (Feminist Press, 2018).

Born and raised in Martinique and now living in Paris, **Gaël Octavia** writes novels, poetry, theater, and short stories. She also paints and makes short films. Inspired by Martinican society, her texts explore themes of family, identity, and the female condition. Her plays have been read and performed in France, the United States, the Caribbean, Reunion Island, and Africa. Her first novel, *La fin de Mame Baby*, received the Wepler Jury Special Mention Award in 2017.

Lynn E. Palermo is a literary and academic translator. Her translation of *Humus* by Fabienne Kanor (University of Virginia Press, 2020) was a finalist for the 2021 National Translation Award. She received a 2018 NEA Translation Grant and a 2016 French Voices Award (with Catherine Dent). Shorter translations have appeared in *World Literature Today*, *Exchanges*, and the *Kenyon Review Online*. Palermo is professor of French Studies at Susquehanna University and does volunteer translation for UN-affiliated organizations.

Lucy Scott is a translator of Caribbean literature written in Dutch and French. Her short story and essay translations thus far have appeared in *Shenandoah: The Washington and Lee Review* and in *Wilderness House Literary Review*. She's the translator of Astrid Roemer's *On a Woman's Madness* (Two Lines Press, 2023) and *Off-White* (Two Lines Press, forthcoming 2024).

CALICO

The Calico Series, published biannually by Two Lines Press, captures vanguard works of translated literature in stylish, collectible editions. Each Calico is a vibrant snapshot that explores one aspect of our present moment, offering the voices of previously inaccessible, highly innovative writers from around the world today.